MARRY
MOTHER

Christine Nostlinger

Translated by Anthea Bell

Beaver Books

A Beaver Book
Published by Arrow Books Limited
62–65 Chandos Place, London, WC2N 4NW

An imprint of Century Hutchinson Ltd

London Melbourne Sydney Auckland
Johannesburg and agencies throughout
the world

First published in English by Andersen Press 1978
This translation © Andersen Press 1978
Originally published in German as *Ein Mann fur Mama*
by Verlag Friedrich Oetinger, Hamburg, 1972

Beaver edition 1986

Printed and bound in Great Britain by
Anchor Brendon Ltd, Tiptree, Essex

ISBN 09 942160 7

1

There was a rose bed in the garden. A round bed, full of rose bushes with yellow roses on them. Grandmother said they were tea roses, though they were not the colour of tea, nor could you make tea out of their leaves. (Great-aunt Alice was always saying, 'What's in a name?' and she had a point there.)

Sue was walking slowly round the rose bed. Sue's full name was Susanna Alice Henrietta Carolina Kaufmann.

Sue walked round the rose bed with her hands clasped behind her back and her head thrust forward. She was making up poetry. Sue often made up poetry. She had once had a fat pink exercise book with a cover saying:

POEMS   *By Susanna Kaufmann*

Sue used to write down her best poems in the pink exercise book, in beautiful ornate handwriting. But then her sister found the book and read the poems out loud to the whole family. She stood in the middle of the sitting room, arms outstretched, shouting, 'Listen to this, everyone! The latest masterpiece by that famous young poetess Susanna Alice Henrietta Carolina Kaufmann, "The Black People".' Here Sue's sister paused dramatically and rolled her eyes. 'Silence, please!'

Sue tried to snatch the book away, but as her sister was a good deal taller she couldn't. Her sister held the book above her head, reading out loud:

'The Black People.
The black people in Africa get plenty of sun.
Otherwise they do not have much fun.'

After that Sue kept her poems in her head. She determined never to put a single word of poetry down on paper ever again. She wasn't going to have people laughing at her! Sue's father had said he liked her poems, but that didn't count, because he wasn't here. He did not live in this house with its garden and the rose bed full of tea roses. Father was still living in their old apartment in another part of the city of Vienna, all by himself, except for Philip the cat. Sue's mother said they had not brought Philip with them because cats are fonder of places than people, but Sue was not so sure. She knew Philip had always liked Father best, and Sue was glad Philip had not come with them. Great-aunt Alice would have plagued the life out of the poor animal. Sue was sure she'd have brushed him every day, and dusted him with her feather duster, and washed his paws when he came in from the garden. This was a very clean house: before you came indoors you had to scrape your feet on the scraper outside for two whole minutes, looking like a horse pawing the ground asking for sugar. Sue did not think Philip would have stood for that.

The house belonged to Grandmother, or maybe to Grandmother and Great-aunt Alice, it was difficult to say for sure. Great-grandfather's will had not been quite clear about it, so Aunt Alice claimed the house belonged to her, while Grandmother said Aunt Alice was talking nonsense, it was perfectly obvious the house was hers.

In reply, Aunt Alice used to whisper, 'Our poor dear papa must be turning in his grave!'

Thinking about Father and their old apartment, and hearing the church clock strike six, Sue made up this poem:

> Back at home
> at six o'clock
> the dogs meet
> out in the street.
> People take them for a walk.
> They sometimes stop to talk.
> Even in the rain
> dogs need exercise just the same.
> I like the people you meet
> with their dogs in the street
> back at home.

Not bad, Sue thought, not bad at all. She started learning the poem off by heart, but she was interrupted by Aunt Alice, who looked out of the middle window of the sitting room and shouted, 'Susanna, it's getting chilly and you've been out there too long. Discretion is the better part of valour. Come indoors at once!'

Sue went indoors. It was no good trying to stand up to Aunt Alice; she had nerves of steel. If Sue had not gone indoors, Aunt Alice would have stayed at the window, scolding her and quoting at least ten proverbs. And when Grandmother and Mother and Aunt Irma came home, Aunt Alice would spend the whole evening telling them, 'So I stood there at the window—a voice crying in the wilderness! I stood there for a whole hour, but would she come in? Oh, dear me, no, she doesn't take any notice of *me!*

'You mark my words, Susanna,' she would add, turning to Sue, 'pride goes before a fall!'

And Grandmother would say, 'Oh, really, Alice, don't you even know how to handle a little girl?'

And Aunt Irma would say, 'Leave the poor child alone!'

7

And Mother would say, 'What do you mean, poor child? Poor child, indeed! Lots of other children would be glad to be in her shoes!'

And Aunt Irma would say, 'A proper home with a father and a mother is what a child needs most.' She would emphasize the word 'father'.

And then Mother would say that wasn't her doing, and Aunt Irma couldn't talk, she'd never been married herself.

And then Aunt Alice would put her arm round Mother's shoulders and say, 'There, there, Caroline, men were deceivers ever!'

And Aunt Irma would laugh, sarcastically, and Grandmother would say, 'That is quite enough of that!'

But in the end they would all finish up blaming Sue for spoiling their evening.

Sue knew word for word how this kind of conversation went, and as she hated every minute of it she decided she'd better go indoors. First, however, she snapped the stem of Grandmother's best tea rose. It will be all withered by tomorrow morning, she thought.

She snapped it even though she liked the yellow tea roses, and just now she had nothing against Grandmother.

Sue was sitting on the pale blue sofa, the one Aunt Alice called a chaise longue. There was a small round table with only one leg in front of the chaise longue: a round, fat leg right in the middle of the table. You had to be careful not to kick it, because the table was very valuable. The valuable table was covered by a silk cloth with a long fringe. Sue began plaiting the fringe into tight little plaits.

'Susanna, please!' wailed Aunt Alice. 'If you want to plait something, plait your doll's hair!'

'I'm too old for dolls,' said Sue.

'Then you're to old to plait that fringe,' said Aunt Alice.

'Yes, Aunt Alice,' muttered Sue, undoing the plaits again.

Great-aunt Alice walked round the sitting room, pulling things straight, pushing other things into place. She re-arranged the curtain folds, and the lace runners on the chests of drawers. She moved the television set a centimetre to the left and the standard lamp with the frilly shade a centimetre to the right. She placed the fruit bowl in the exact middle of the table, and she moved the small rug till it was at right angles with the big rug. The only things Aunt Alice left alone were the rubber plant and the Busy Lizzie. 'The less you touch indoor plants the better,' Aunt Alice used to say.

'Where's J?' asked Sue.

J was short for Julia, Sue's sister. She was fourteen, four years older than Sue.

Great-aunt Alice straightened the tasselled cover on the piano and shrugged her shoulders.

'How should I know?' she grumbled. 'No one ever tells me anything!' However, she added, 'She went to see her friend. Someone called Erna. At least, I heard her talking to this Erna on the phone, but don't ask me if that's where she really went. That girl is always using the phone! Our telephone bills have doubled since you came to live here!'

Sue looked at Aunt Alice, and her thin, white, permed hair, and her little eyes, grey as the river Danube, and her double chin. Silly old cow, thought Sue.

Great-aunt Alice shut the middle window of the sitting room.

'Chilly,' she muttered. 'Very chilly for early September.'

'It's twenty-three degrees,' said Sue, nudging the small rug with her foot, so that *something* would be slightly out of place. Good, it was crooked now! It was even rucked up.

Aunt Alice did not notice. She was looking at the road

9

outside the garden.

'Oh, really! It's infuriating!' she snorted.

'What's infuriating?' asked Sue. She knew quite well Aunt Alice had not seen anything really infuriating.

'That dreadful man Meier!' said Aunt Alice crossly. 'Parking his car outside our fence again!'

'Is it forbidden?' asked Sue. She liked Mr Meier, especially when he parked his car outside Grandmother's house.

'Not exactly forbidden,' said Aunt Alice, getting all worked up. 'But it's an unwritten law! A fence belongs to a house, and the bit of pavement outside the fence belongs to the fence, and the bit of road next to that bit of pavement belongs to the pavement, so it belongs to the house!'

'You'd better explain that to Mr Meier,' suggested Sue. Aunt Alice looked horrified.

'Me, approach that dreadful man? Certainly not! He just grins at one in the most impertinent way! Well, pride comes before a fall! He who laughs last laughs longest! Anyway, I don't own a car. It's up to your mother or your grandmother or your aunt to tackle him. *They* have cars.'

Sue realized that she could not bear Aunt Alice's company a moment longer. She got up off the chaise longue and left the room. She went into the kitchen, opened the kitchen window and climbed out into the garden. Then she ran over to the fence between Grandmother's garden and the garden next door. She scrambled up on the wire netting of the fence, so that she could see over the bushes the other side, and called, 'Benny! Benny! Hi, Benny!'

She did not call very loud; she didn't want Great-aunt Alice hearing her, because Benny, otherwise Benjamin Meier, was the son of that dreadful man Meier who kept parking his car outside Grandmother's house, and Aunt

Alice did not like Sue mixing with the dreadful man's son. 'Like father, like son,' Aunt Alice used to say. She had a proverb for every occasion.

Since Sue did not call very loud, Benny didn't hear her, but his dog, a fat old dachshund called Mr Joseph, came waddling over.

'Hi, Mr Joseph,' said Sue. 'Is Benny in?'

Mr Joseph barked.

Sue decided that meant 'Yes'. She climbed the fence and went over to Benny's house, with Mr Joseph wheezing along after her. Mr Joseph had asthma, and could not run very fast.

While Sue is sitting in her friend Benny's kitchen, eating salami and drinking coca-cola and discussing the awfulness of great-aunts (it was a rather one-sided discussion, since Benny, not having any great-aunts, could only listen), I will try to explain Sue's family to you.

First there was Grandmother. Her name was Henrietta Buchinger. (Sue got her third name from Grandmother.) Grandmother was about sixty, very tall and rather fat, and she had a deep voice. Sue's father called her 'the Sergeant-Major', and tried to keep out of her way. A family visit once a year at Easter was quite enough for him, he said. However, Grandmother was always very nice to him. She had a shop, where she sold all sorts of odd things: milking stools, butter churns, curry-combs for horses, ladles with wooden handles, salt cellars, brass flatirons, copper kettles.

Then there was Great-aunt Alice, whom we have just met. She didn't go out to work, she kept house for Grandmother. Besides dusting things and putting things straight, she could make raspberry jam with cognac, and cakes with lemon icing. Aunt Alice could not stand men. Not just that dreadful man Meier, she didn't like any men at all. (A man had let her down almost half a century ago. At the time, Aunt Alice had decided to marry this man, but he had been against it.)

Grandmother's own husband had been dead for years. There was a picture of him in the sitting room, but he is not important to this story. (In fact he was only important to Aunt Alice, who dusted him three times a day.)

Grandmother had two daughters. One was Caroline, who was Sue's mother. The other was Aunt Irma. Aunt Irma was just thirty, but she looked more like twenty. She was slim and blonde and she had blue eyes and a pretty little nose. Sue once wrote a poem about Aunt Irma:

> Aunt Irma has lovely hair.
> People stop and stare
> when they see Aunt Irma's hair.
> They also stare at her eyes
> which are blue as the skies.
> It is a great pity
> the rest of my family are not so pretty.

Aunt Irma helped Grandmother in the shop (Father used to describe it as 'a junk shop'). She always looked after the gentlemen customers. If a gentleman came into Grandmother's shop and looked into Aunt Irma's blue eyes he was ready to believe anything. She could convince him a flowered butter churn was just what he needed for an umbrella stand; he couldn't imagine how he had ever got on without an elephant's foot, and of course he realized that a milking stool is a particularly comfortable form of seating, and every man of the world requires an elaborately carved meerschaum pipe hanging over his bed. If a gentleman was very hard to please, and looked like going away without buying anything, Aunt Irma would smile at him. She had two dimples on each cheek and a dimple in her chin, and when she smiled like that, and went on looking at the customer with her deep blue eyes, he suddenly realized that a brass plant holder shaped like an iron, for growing cactuses in, was exactly what his wife wanted for her birthday.

Sue's mother was rather older than Aunt Irma, and not quite so slim and blonde and blue-eyed. She was a buyer for the Soho Lady boutique. It was hard work: Sue's mother had to guess what sort of skirts and sweaters would be in fashion next year, and how many coats the Soho Lady would sell, and she needed to know in advance whether their customers would want check coats or striped coats.

Sue's sister Julia, J for short, was pretty. If she put her mind to it, she looked like growing up to be as slim and blonde and blue-eyed as Aunt Irma.

Until two months before, Sue had lived with her mother and father and J and Philip the cat in a third-floor apartment in a big building in another part of Vienna. Then, two months ago, they had gone on holiday to Yugoslavia—all except the cat, of course; he stayed at home, with the caretaker of the building looking after him.

The holiday began quite normally, with a slight family quarrel, because the cases weren't big enough and J wanted to take so many things with her. Then there was another, medium-sized family quarrel at the airport, over who had the passports and the air tickets. And Mother was annoyed because Father bought four large packs of cigarettes in the duty-free shop, where you can get things cheaper, but no Dior perfume.

However, quarrels of this kind were nothing unusual in the Kaufmann family, so Sue didn't worry about them. She got into the plane and spent the whole flight from Vienna to Split in Yugoslavia eating the enormous tray of

13

refreshments the stewardess brought her. She looked out of the window, admiring the mountains of rosy pink clouds and thinking about the seaside, the sun, and the water melons she'd be eating, and trying to remember if she'd left one of her frogman flippers under her bed at home instead of packing it in her case.

By the time the plane landed in Split Sue had finished the tray of refreshments and decided where the flipper was. 'J, I've left one of my flippers at home,' she told her sister.

J shrugged her shoulders. 'I've left the tops of both my bikinis in the bathroom,' she whispered.

'Are they still cross with each other?' Sue pointed to Mother and Father, who were waiting at the baggage-claim.

'Looks like it,' said J.

'Why does Mother want Dior perfume on holiday anyway?' asked Sue. 'The water would just wash it off!'

'Well, why does Father want so many cigarettes?' asked J. 'He can't smoke two at once!'

We might as well go to Sue's diary for the story of the Kaufmann family's Yugoslavian holiday. Sue's diary had squared paper, because it was really supposed to be for arithmetic. Her mother had bought it before they left, saying, 'Sue, you really must do some arithmetic these holidays. You're going to secondary school in the autumn, and you know arithmetic's your weak point.'

Sue had no intention of ruining her holidays by doing arithmetic. She wrote DIARY on the cover of the book, and conscientiously put down everything that happened to her on holiday. (Only the things she thought really important, of course.)

We can skip the first three pages of the diary, which are about a shopping trip to buy a pair of flippers and a bikini, along with a description of the family's hotel

14

rooms, and a description of the head waiter in the dining room, and an account of the waves two metres tall and how Sue did three perfect dives. (Strictly speaking, that was not quite correct; the waves were only half a metre tall, and Sue did not keep her legs straight when she dived.)

We will begin on the fourth day of the holiday.

2

5th July

J either has adenoids or she's getting a cold. She snores so loud at night it wakes me up. It woke me up last night, and I got up and went out on the balcony, because I once read somewhere that it's a marvellous feeling to be out on your own in the middle of the night and hear the sound of the sea. And the sea is right outside our balcony, only I couldn't hear it because it was so calm. I was going to start making up a poem about a calm sea when I heard voices on the balcony next to ours. It's Mother and Father's balcony, and they were quarrelling again. I don't think quarrelling is all that bad; I mean, J and I often quarrel, but we're quite fond of each other. But the way Mother and Father have been quarrelling lately isn't really funny.

Emmy at school told me her parents shout at each other when they're having a fight, so loud most of the people in the building can hear them. Mother and Father don't shout, but they sound very bitter and sort of venomous. They hiss at each other, the way snakes are supposed to, and they've been quarrelling about things that happened ages ago. Last night I heard Mother saying how mean of Father it was to go away on holiday by himself ten years ago, when I was a baby. And Father told Mother how mean it was of *her* to throw Uncle Jonny out of our apartment seven years ago. Then they said a whole lot of things about each other that weren't true, or only partly

16

true. I know Mother does look rather funny with her night cream on her face, but not really like Dracula. And Father doesn't go out with his friends every single night leaving Mother all alone. Mother doesn't make a mess of absolutely everything she cooks, either. Sometimes she can cook some quite nice things. And the money Father earns isn't just a miserable pittance; Emmy at school would like it if her father earned as much as mine. And Father doesn't goggle at pretty blondes *every* time he sees one. And Mother doesn't have a headache every day. Only about every other day, if that.

I felt like climbing over to Mother and Father's balcony to tell them they were both wrong. I felt like telling them all the things they tell J and me when *we* quarrel. Only I bet they'd have said it was none of my business and sent me back to bed.

I went quietly round and had a peep into their room just now, before I started writing. They're still asleep. They look quite peaceful when they're asleep. J's asleep too. I'm going down to have breakfast.

Now it's evening. J is in bed reading a thriller. It must be exciting, because she's biting her nails. It was hot today. Mother spent the day in bed, because her constitution can't stand the heat. Father wasn't very good company either. He lay in the shade and read and smoked. When I asked him anything he didn't answer, just growled like an old dog. Neither of them came in to lunch, so J and I had the table to ourselves. The nice young waiter, the one with black hair flopping over on his forehead, asked, 'Mother and Father not good?' (He meant: were they ill?) I nodded to the nice waiter and told him, 'No, Mother and Father not good.'

That made J and me laugh, but we didn't really think it was all that funny. We had two cokes each, and we drank to each other, and J said, 'Cheers, Sue. Oh, what a day we're having!' And she muttered under her breath, 'Marvellous parents we picked, I must say!'

I said we hadn't picked our own parents, and J said did I have to take everything so literally, and then we started quarrelling too, and J marched out of the dining room.

I spent the afternoon on my own. I went down to the beach to see if I could make friends with any children, but I couldn't find anyone my age. Then I sat down beside a toddler making sand castles, but all the toddler could say was, 'Da, da, ba, ba,' and when I picked up his bucket to help him make sand castles he yelled blue murder.

7th July

I didn't write anything in this diary yesterday. Yesterday was a nice day. Father and Mother are friends again. At least, *I* think so, but J says I'm imagining things. Well, anyway, they weren't quarrelling, that's the main thing. Our hotel is quite a long way from Split, standing all by itself, and it's half an hour's walk to the nearest village. The trouble is the hotel always sells out of my favourite ice cream flavours by about the middle of the day; after that they only have vanilla and hazelnut left, and I don't like them. So yesterday we walked to the village with Mother and Father for an ice cream. But the road to the village is pretty stony, and Father said it was a nuisance not having a car here.

In the afternoon Father took me and J sailing. We sail on the river at home in Vienna, but it's a lot more difficult sailing on the sea. It was nice, all the same, because Father had cheered up and he was fun to be with. That evening we stayed up late. We sat in the bar out of doors where they have a band playing and a girl singer. She was a very beautiful black girl, but thank goodness Father didn't say how pretty she was, he only said she sang too loud. Then we went for a walk in the moonlight, on the landing stage that goes right out into the sea. You could only walk along quite a narrow bit of it, because there were people sitting cuddling each other both sides of the landing stage.

At breakfast today Mother and Father were still friends. Mother buttered Father's roll for him, and Father ordered Mother an orange juice, which is always a good sign.

After breakfast we went down to the beach, and Father did get rather cross because of all the stuff Mother was taking. He said she had enough equipment there for a two-week expedition. But Mother doesn't enjoy going on the beach without a lot of stuff. She had Father loaded up like a camel, with three airbeds, a sunshade, an air pillow, three bath towels, a transistor radio, a tin of biscuits and a plastic bag of grapes. (Later some ants got into the biscuit tin, and J cried because she thought she might have swallowed one.)

Mother was carrying a bag of sun-tan creams and so on. A special sun oil for me, because I still have a child's skin. A special cream for J, because she has a teenager's skin. And several different tubes and jars for Mother, who needs a lotion for her face, a spray for her legs, and a sort of jelly for her tummy.

Mother was very cheerful, and when she's cheerful she goes all poetic and makes up poetic comparisons. J joins in. They were both sitting on the red airbed, the big one which took quarter of an hour for Father to blow up. They were rubbing sun-tan cream into each other and admiring the beach. Like this:

Mother: 'Oh, look at the sea! Like blue silk!'
J: 'And the little clouds! Like whipped cream!'
Mother: 'And see the sun! Like an orange!'

19

J: 'And the little children! Brown as Africans!'

They went on like this for about an hour, and Father was looking more and more dismal all the time. He doesn't go in for poetic comparisons. He had his revenge at lunch. When a lady in a blue, silky dress passed our table he said out loud, 'Oh, look! A dress like the sea!'

Then the waiter brought us a tart covered with whipped cream. Father looked soulfully at the whipped cream and said, 'Like the little clouds in the sky!'

Mother didn't want any cream tart because of being ten kilos overweight (Mother, not the tart). The waiter brought her an orange. Father narrowed his eyes, gazed at the orange and whispered, 'An orange! Just like the sun!'

'Fred, stop that!' Mother hissed. Father said why should he stop? He was only trying to be poetic, like Mother down on the beach. He didn't stop, either. Yesterday a French couple who are black arrived at the hotel, and they have the table next to ours. Father looked at the two black French people and said, 'So brown! Just like the dear little children!'

Mother hissed that either Father left the dining room at once, or she did. Father hissed back that if was no fun being with people who couldn't take a joke, and he did leave the dining room. Mother was furious, so she said I was picking my nose and I'd better get out too. I didn't mind. I'd finished eating, and my bottle of coke was empty, and J still had half of hers left. It's maddening watching someone else put back her coke when you're still thirsty yourself.

8th July

It's late in the evening. J has gone to sleep over her book. She's snoring, with her mouth open. She looks very silly like that. No one would know she's a pretty girl in the

20

daytime. Well, perhaps I only think that because we've been getting on each other's nerves all day. Not exactly quarrelling, just snapping at each other. I suppose I did keep on at her a bit, to be honest. But J does act in a very silly way sometimes.

For one thing, she kept on calling Mother 'Mama' all day. She thought it sounded posh, and I know why she wanted to sound posh too. Three airbeds away from us on the beach there's a family with a tall, fair-haired boy. J fancies him, that's why she was trying to sound posh. You could tell it wasn't for our benefit, it was aimed at the tall, fair boy.

And for another thing, she put her ceramic ring on her second toe, and wound her little gold necklace round her ankle, and she sat there admiring her foot.

And the third thing that made me furious was when I wanted her to come in the water with me, or go to buy an ice. I mean, what's a sister for, anyway? But J just lay there. 'You go, little sister!' she said. That annoyed me worst of all. Whenever she wants to impress someone, like that fair-haired boy today, she thinks treating me like a baby sounds very sophisticated.

The tall fair-haired boy has a little brother, who's rather sweet. I was so bored I played in the sand with the little brother. We dug a long ditch, and the tall fair boy came and helped us. Actually he's not bad. We went in the water together. He can swim like a fish, and very fast too. He brought up three shells from the bottom for me. He's in the sixth form at school, and his father is an ear, nose and throat doctor in Graz, and he specializes in thyroid operations; there are lots of people with thyroid trouble in Graz because of the high iodine content in the water. The tall fair boy told me all about it. His name's Peter.

Then J was annoyed with me because I'd made friends with the tall fair boy and she hadn't. Silly fool, all she had

21

to do was take her ring and her necklace off her foot and come and play in the sand too.

And J is annoyed with Father as well, because he said she looked like a tame canary with that chain round her ankle. (Canaries often do have rings round their legs.) And I'm annoyed with Mother because she said I pick my nose and I have no idea how to behave.

So now our family's divided right down the middle.

Yesterday, before we were divided down the middle, we'd decided to go to Split by bus on Sunday, which is tomorrow. I wonder if we'll be going now or not? I expect we will. When Mother and Father promise to do something they usually stick to it, even if they've had a fight in the meantime. There are supposed to be lots of things to see in Split. For instance, there's an underground palace. I hope they have a big market selling carved wooden things and rolls of material and shoes and water melons. I like big, noisy, cheerful markets. I could stay there while Father goes to look at the underground palace.

9th July (Early in the morning, before breakfast. My tummy's rumbling.)

Yes, we *are* going to Split. Our bus leaves at nine. I'm supposed to hurry, but J's been in the bathroom for an hour doing things to her face, so I don't see how I can. The bathroom's tiny; it won't take two people at once, and if J is much longer I won't even be able to wash.

We've slept off being annoyed with each other; we're friends again now.

Mother has just knocked on our door and told me I must wear socks. I asked why I had to wear socks. She said I asked too many questions. I can't stand it when she says that!

Now Father has just knocked at our door to tell us it's

22

time for breakfast. So I'll have to go down without washing. I'm not putting any socks on either, because I can only find my green socks, and they don't go with my red dress or my blue sandals.

J is finally coming out of the bathroom. She says I'm a dirty pig because I haven't washed, but I'm not going to answer back. I don't want to quarrel again.

9th July (Evening)

We went to Split. What a day! I'm all confused. I'm dead tired too. It must be about midnight; the band down on the beach has just stopped playing. I'm not sure exactly how late it is, because my watch has gone wrong. In fact everything has gone wrong.

J is sitting on the balcony. She says she isn't going to bed at all, as if that would make any difference. I asked her if it was all my fault. J said, 'No, it wasn't your fault, you were just the trigger factor.'

I'm not sure what she meant by that, but it sounds comforting. I'd rather be a trigger factor than feel it was all my fault.

I'm going to bed now.

I'm looking forward to my dreams. When I'm sad or upset in the day I always have good dreams at night. Lovely, blissful, happy dreams.

Tonight I ought to have an extra-lovely, blissful, happy dream!

10th July (Morning)

J is packing her case. Mother is packing hers. And then Mother is going to the airport to see if there are three seats available on a flight home. Our tickets are really booked for the 28th July. Mother will have to settle things with the hotel, too, because we'd booked our rooms until the

28th as well, and paid in advance, so now Mother wants some of the money back. Settling things with the hotel isn't easy, because the staff only speak Serbo-Croat and French, and Mother doesn't speak either.

Thank goodness I don't have to pack my case, because I'd hardly unpacked any of it yet. So I'm sitting on the balcony, and I've got time to write down what happened in Split yesterday. It was like this:

We got to the bus stop at nine, so as to be sure we didn't miss the bus, but then we had to wait an hour, because the buses here don't run when the timetable says they will. There were lots of people at the bus stop, and it was terribly hot. Father kept saying he was never going on holiday without a car again. Finally the bus came. I've never seen a bus like it. It rattled and clattered, because there were so many screws loose or missing. Round the seats and the windows and the driver's cab. The metal plates on the floor were loose too; that was why the bus clattered so much. But after a bit you didn't notice, because so many people got in there wasn't any room left for the pieces of bus to rattle.

The bus stopped about every three minutes. Each time I thought: they couldn't even squeeze a mouse into this bus now! But each time I was wrong, because at least another five people got in.

Mother was beside me, and she groaned and said she thought she was going to faint, and Father said that would be the first time she had fainted standing up, because there wasn't any room to fall down. So Mother didn't faint, she just moaned quietly to herself.

I was all right, even though I could only stand on one leg because I happened to have taken one foot off the floor of the bus for a moment, and when I tried to put it down again there wasn't any room left for it. But right in front of me was a basket of grapes, and the lady carrying

24

the basket made signs to me to help myself. There was a nice smell in the bus, too, the sort I like. It smelt of grapes and dust and tomatoes and bread-and-dripping. There was a kind of wet-dog smell too, though there weren't any dogs in the bus.

It's only twenty kilometres from the hotel to Split, but the drive took nearly an hour. When we got out J cried. She'd been standing squeezed between two net bags of tomatoes on the bus, and tomatoes squash easily. J had red marks on the back and front of her dress, and there were tomato pips sticking to it.

Mother took a few deep breaths and then she felt better. We walked along the narrow old streets. Mother kept saying, 'Oh!' and 'Look!' and 'How picturesque!' I looked through the gates and windows of the houses we were passing, to see what they were like inside. They looked much worse than Emmy's apartment. And I remember Mother fetching me from Emmy's apartment one day, and saying on the way home the conditions some poor people had to live in were quite scandalous. She didn't say 'Oh!' and 'Look!' and 'How picturesque!' that time.

Later on we passed buildings that looked just like our apartment building in Vienna, and Mother said it was disgraceful, people putting up these eyesores all over the place, and it ought to be forbidden. Father said the people of Split weren't going to go on living in their old hovels just on account of Mother's cultural preferences.

J didn't say anything. She was dawdling along behind us, trying to get the marks off her dress.

Father went to see the underground palace, and we went into a café near the ruins, with tables in the open air. We ate ices and drank coca-cola and admired the ruins; admiring ruins is quite comfortable if you can do it sitting down. By now J had scratched all the tomato pips off, so she had time to say 'Oh!' and 'Look!' too.

Then Father came out of the underground palace, and paid the bill, and we went to the market. Mother wanted to buy presents to take home. A fruit bowl for Grandmother, a wooden stork for Great-aunt Alice, and a leather bottle for Aunt Irma. And a leather coat for herself, because they're cheap in Yugoslavia. And she wanted a Turkish coffee mill too. J wanted a pair of sandals and a peasant blouse and a red cap with a black tassel. And Father didn't want to pay for all these things. Mother said they were very good value, and she ought to know, being a fashion buyer herself. Father said the question was not whether they were good value, it was whether we needed them. He and Mother said quite a lot more, but there was so much noise in the market that all I caught was: 'Typical—spending money like water!' and: 'You grudge me the slightest pleasure!'

Then we made our way through all the people over to the bus stop. Father was in front, J and Mother were following him, and I was behind them. I had a stitch, so I was walking slowly. Then all of a sudden I couldn't see J and Mother any more, or Father either. I was in the middle of a crowd of old ladies with black scarves on their heads selling melons and sweet peppers and tomatoes. I felt frightened and started to run, right through the crowd of old ladies. But I must have taken the wrong turning; all the roads looked the same. I went all over the place, but I couldn't find the bus stop. Then I ran into a lady, and she could see I was scared, and thank goodness she knew a little German. She took me to the square where the bus stop was. But unfortunately it was the other side of the square, and the lights were red. When I looked across the square I could see Mother's lilac straw hat and J's pink straw hat disappearing into the bus. Then the bus door closed and it drove off.

I felt very sorry for myself. I was in a foreign city,

without any Yugoslavian money at all, and the only Serbian word I know is 'Sladoled', which means ice cream. The thing I really couldn't understand was how my family could have gone without me. (J explained later: Father got into the bus first, thinking I was with Mother, and Mother got into the bus last, thinking I was with Father. Mother couldn't see Father because of all the people in between them, and for the same reason Father couldn't see Mother.)

But I wasn't to know that. I cried. Finally a policeman came along and said if I would stop crying and tell him all about it, slowly, he could understand me. I stopped crying, and I did tell him all about it, slowly, and he did understand me. He took me to the police station, and telephoned some other police stations and the hotel where we were staying. Then he told me, 'There, little lady! Father and Mother soon know. Soon fetch!'

But it wasn't as simple as that. The police knew, and so did the secretary at the hotel, but my family did not know, not yet. Because when the bus reached the hotel Father got out first again and Mother got out last. By the time Mother and J were out of the bus, Father had disappeared round the bend in the road, and he was out of sight among the olive trees. He didn't go into the hotel, he went into the café on the beach, and of course no one knew about me in the café. Mother and J went into the café too, but they sat at a different table, because they were annoyed with Father about the things he didn't buy. All the same, it gradually dawned on them that someone was missing. Mother began to worry. She sent J over to ask Father where I was. (When they're on bad terms J always has to act as interpreter.) So then it turned out I'd disappeared. And Mother and Father were angrier with each other than ever, and they both said it was the other one's fault.

I still didn't know anything about all this. It was very

27

boring, waiting at the police station. At last Father came to fetch me, and we took a taxi; the driver said it would cost a lot, but Father said he didn't care, he'd had quite enough bus travel for one day. He asked me if I'd been scared, and I told a lie and said no, it had been quite fun, so then Father felt better.

Mother was waiting outside the hotel. She laid the emotion on very thick. She ran to me and hugged me and sobbed. It was like a film. All the other hotel guests standing around acted like people in a film too. Mother stroked my hair and whispered, 'My poor, dear little love!'

Father hissed at Mother to stop play-acting. Mother went on stroking my hair and she shouted that Father was brutal and callous and he was trampling her loving, maternal heart underfoot.

Then they ordered supper for me. The waiter brought me a steak and a piece of tart and a coke. Mother sat on my right and Father sat on my left.

Mother said, 'There, darling, eat it up, you must be starving!'

Father said, 'Leave any you don't want!'

Mother said, 'Well, it's not likely you won't want your favourite meal, is it?'

Father said, 'She can leave it if she wants to.'

Mother said, 'And look at that delicious tart!'

Father said, 'Looks heavy to me.'

Then I put my knife and fork down on the table, and I stood up so suddenly that the bottle of coke fell over, and I ran out of the dining room.

J was sitting on the balcony. She was crying; she said she just couldn't stand it, having parents like ours. I soon went to sleep, because I was so tired.

And then, this morning, Father had gone! He'd packed his things in the night and left. We don't even know *where* he's gone. J says it's horrible of him, and she never wants to see him again, after the way he's treated us. Maybe she's right. At least, I know Mother wouldn't have run off and left us here. But I love Father all the same.

I'll have to stop now. The taxi is coming in ten minutes to take us to the airport.

I don't really understand why we're going home. I mean, we could stay and lie on the beach and eat ice cream and go bathing without Father, and he might come back in a few days' time. But Mother won't hear of it.

Perhaps Father will be waiting at the airport when we get back to Vienna. That would be nice.

3

The entry for the 10th July is the last one in Sue's diary. After that the exercise book was turned into a rough book for school, containing several maths problems, a number of pictures of teachers' heads in profile, and some charts to help Sue get through boring lessons. Each chart consisted of fifty little squares, outlined in red felt pen, so that Sue could sit and cross out the little squares, one a minute, to pass the time until the bell went.

Which means I must go on with the story myself.

Sue, J and Mother flew back to Vienna on the midday plane. Sue didn't feel like eating the refreshments the stewardess brought. She stared out of the window. There were white clouds underneath the plane, and pink clouds beside it. The clouds looked thick and solid. Sue felt you could walk on them and not fall through.

Sue imagined herself walking through the clouds alone, shimmering with gold, bathed in a pink glow. She was just wondering what sort of clothes you would wear for a walk among the clouds, and had decided on a white batiste nightie with an embroidered hem, when the stewardess's voice came over the loudspeaker. 'Please fasten your seat belts.' The No Smoking sign at the front of the plane lit up.

'Nearly there,' said Mother.

Father was not waiting at the airport; Sue looked hard, but she couldn't see him anywhere.

Father was at home in the apartment. When Sue, J and

Mother got home they found him lying on the sitting room sofa, drinking beer and reading the paper, with Philip the cat sitting on his stomach. The ash tray was full of cigarette ends, and there was a good deal of smoke drifting about the room.

'Hullo there!' said Father. 'But why did you . . . I was just going to . . . . '

'Hullo there, indeed!' said Mother. 'You were just going to what? You're not about to say you were on your way back to Split, are you?'

Father put his beer glass down on the floor.

'Well, actually I was,' he said. 'I was just going to finish this beer, and then—'

'Finish that beer!' screeched Mother. 'It's the most unheard-of thing I ever heard of in all my life!'

Philip the cat mewed. He was trembling all over. Cats don't like people screeching. Sue went over and stroked Philip. She stroked Father a little, too.

'Is Mother very cross?' asked Father quietly.

Sue nodded. Father grinned.

'Why did you go?' asked Sue.

Father whispered back, 'Couldn't stand it any longer! Four days and four nights quarrelling without a break . . . too much for any man!'

Sue nodded again, as if she understood, though she did not really understand at all. Why exactly had Father spent four days and four nights quarrelling? Didn't he know it takes two to make a quarrel?

While Sue was nodding and stroking Philip and Father, Mother was on the phone. Sue couldn't hear what she was saying, because she had taken the phone into the bedroom, ruthlessly jamming the flex in the bedroom door as she closed it. When someone takes the phone into another room it usually bodes no good. Sue glanced at the flex. She had a feeling it might be a good idea to cut it. But

31

you don't just go around cutting telephone flexes. Indeed, you don't very often go around doing any of the things you'd really like to.

Mother came back out of the bedroom with the phone and slammed it down on the coffee table. In so doing, she stumbled over the flex and nearly fell flat. Father grinned again. Mother gave him a fierce look, then she went back into the bedroom and started taking her dresses and underclothes out of the wardrobe. She dumped them on the double bed. She went into the girls' room and came back, breathing hard, with a huge armful of clothes, pyjama legs and blouse sleeves dangling round her. She went back and forth, collecting things, until there was a positive mountain of dresses and skirts and underclothes and shoes on the double bed. And she kept muttering to herself, 'It's best this way! The best thing for all of us!'

She sounded as if she were trying to learn something off by heart.

Sue realized their winter clothes had been added to the mountain on the double bed too.

Then Mother phoned Mr Berger, who ran a removals business in the building next door. 'Yes, I need you at once,' Mother shouted down the phone. 'Now! Yes, yes, the minibus will do. That's right, to my mother's, in Hitzing.' (Hitzing is a suburb of Vienna.)

Mother's intentions were only too obvious; a dimmer child than Sue would have realized what was up, and Sue was not dim. But still, she asked Father, 'What's Mother doing?'

'I think you're moving out,' Father said.

'But I don't want to move out!' whispered Sue. '*Do* something!'

'Like what?' asked Father.

'Say you're sorry!'

'But I'm not sorry.'

'Well, you could say so, couldn't you?'

'No!'

'Please, Father!'

'No!'

Sue stopped stroking Philip and Father and walked away. She would never, never be able to understand how anyone could lie on the sofa, drinking beer and reading the small ads, while his wife got ready to go away with his children.

Mother tried to lure Philip into the cat basket, but he wouldn't go. He jumped off Father's stomach, scuttled into the bedroom and got under the bed. Mother went after him and tried to entice him out. At this, Father put down his paper. 'Caroline!' he shouted. 'Leave that cat alone! He's staying, understand? That's my cat!'

Sue went into the girls' room. She sat down on her bed. J was standing by the window. 'He said Philip was his cat,' Sue said. 'He said Philip's staying.'

'I know,' said J. 'I heard.'

Sue said, 'He could have said we were his children, and we were staying!'

'But he didn't,' said J.

'No, he didn't,' Sue agreed.

Then Mr Berger came. He helped Mother get the mountain of things packed up. J collected their school cases, and the badminton set, and the record player. (The record player really belonged to Father too, but he said nothing about that.)

After Mr Berger had left the apartment for the seventh time with a huge bundle of stuff, he came back and said, 'That's the lot, ma'am.'

'At last!' said Mother. And she muttered quietly, 'It's best this way. The best thing for all of us!' (She knew her lines all right now, she was word-perfect.)

J was already standing at the front door. She looked

very odd, because she had handbags hanging all over her. Three of them were Sue's, seven of them belonged to J, and fourteen of them were Mother's.

'Come along, Sue!' Mother called.

Sue was still in the girls' bedroom. She thought: I must move slowly, very slowly. To give Father time to get back to normal and say he isn't letting us go!

'I need the lavatory,' Sue told Mother.

'Well, hurry up!' said Mother.

Sue went into the lavatory, sat down and waited, but Father did not begin shouting. Mother knocked on the lavatory door. She said no one needed to spend that long in there. Her voice was shrill and trembling. Sue came out of the lavatory, and Mother hustled her out of the hall and to the top of the stairs. The front door of the apartment closed behind them. Not even with a bang, it just closed in a perfectly ordinary way. The staircase looked the same as ever too.

There was a taxi outside the building. Mother told the driver, 'My mother's house!'

The taxi driver grinned. 'Sorry, ma'am, I don't have the pleasure of knowing your mother!'

'Hitzing!' Mother snapped.

The driver started off. Sue felt very envious of him; he was lucky, not knowing Grandmother.

So that is what had happened, and now we can go back to the beginning of the story.

Sue was sitting in her friend Benny's kitchen, explaining grandmothers and great-aunts to Benny, who had none of either. However, he listened sympathetically.

Not far off, in Grandmother's house, Great-aunt Alice was dusting the sitting room furniture yet again with her sky-blue feather duster. This was the third time she had dusted the room that day. The first time she dusted it she used to say, 'Well begun is half done.'

J was just coming in. She asked where Sue was, and Aunt Alice shrugged her shoulders. 'How should I know? No one ever tells me anything,' she said. She added, 'I daresay she went over the fence to see that person.'

J pretended not to know what Aunt Alice meant. 'You mean there's actually a person living next door?' she said.

Great-aunt Alice suggested that J might stop to think that she, Aunt Alice, knew all about J's sly little ways. J rolled her eyes despairingly and went into the room she and Sue shared.

Soon afterwards Grandmother's car turned into the road, with Aunt Irma's car right behind it. Grandmother and Aunt Irma were both annoyed to see Mr Meier's car parked outside their house again. They planned revenge. Aunt Irma parked her car so close in front of Mr Meier's car, and Grandmother parked hers so close behind it, that there was no room for him to manoeuvre out. 'That'll show him!' said Grandmother, with satisfaction.

(Aunt Alice, watching from the sitting room window, commented that one learnt from one's mistakes.)

Sue's mother came home too. She was driving an ancient Volkswagen, which she parked further up the road, not wishing to get mixed up in the parking feud.

When Sue scrambled back over the fence, through the kitchen window and into the house, she could hear the massed female voices of the family rising in chorus in the sitting room. Aunt Alice, her voice a descant above all the others, was just proclaiming, 'He who digs a pit for others falls into it himself.'

Sue hoped to sneak past the sitting room door, but it opened, and there was Grandmother standing in the doorway. 'So here the young lady is!' she said. 'And where, pray, has the young lady been? What kept her out so late, eh?'

Sue felt furious. Positively furious. 'Sorry, Sergeant-Major, ma'am!' she said. 'Beg to report I've been visiting the Meiers, Sergeant-Major, ma'am! And Mr Meier sends his regards and says he won't be needing his car till tomorrow evening, so there wasn't any point in it anyway, Sergeant-Major, ma'am!'

Father would have thought that was funny. That dreadful man Meier would probably have thought so too. Benny certainly would! But neither Father, Mr Meier nor Benny was here, so there was nobody to think it funny. Not even Aunt Irma. Or if she did, she wasn't saying so.

Great-aunt Alice said, 'This really is going too far!'

Mother said, 'Sue, you will apologize to Grandmother at once!'

And why did Mother say that? She must know Sue had no intention of apologizing. Sue couldn't have apologized even if she'd wanted to; the words would have stuck in her throat. Once upon a time, before they came to live with Grandmother, Mother would never have demanded an apology from Sue in that tone.

Great-aunt Alice stuck out her double chin and said, 'The impertinence! If she'd called *me* a sergeant-major, Henrietta, she'd have learnt her lesson, I can tell you!'

Grandmother looked sympathetically at Aunt Alice. 'Oh, Alice, don't be silly!' she said. 'No one would ever call you anything higher in rank than a corporal!'

Aunt Alice gasped for air, like a fish which has jumped out of the water by mistake. Her chin sank back into the white lace collar of her blouse, the white lace collar quivered, and she left the sitting room muttering something about thankless children and ingratitude being sharper than the serpent's tooth, and calling no man happy until he is dead. Aunt Irma groaned.

'Can we *never* have a peaceful evening in this house?' J whispered, 'Sue, don't keep picking quarrels.'

36

Mother said, 'Sue, I'm waiting for that apology.'

Grandmother said she did not expect an apology from someone of Sue's immaturity.

Sue stood by the middle window, looking out at the rose bed. Her face was pressed against the pane. A voice behind her said, 'Sue!' twice.

It was probably Mother, but they all had very similar voices. If you didn't look—and Sue was not looking—you couldn't be sure who was speaking. Then she heard footsteps, and the sound of the sitting room door closing.

4

Sue was left alone. Sue thought: Benny's right after all. He had told her he thought there was bound to be a catty atmosphere in a house full of women; women (well, he actually said *females*), women just can't get on together. His father said so.

It's because there are so many women in this house all on top of each other, thought Sue. Not a man among us. That's the trouble. We ought to do something about it. I suppose we can't really throw Grandmother or Aunt Alice or Aunt Irma out, though. It is their house, after all.

So what? So we must get a man into the place. One of them will have to get married. Only which one? Grandmother's too much of a sergeant-major, nobody would have *her*. Great-aunt Alice? No, nobody would have her either! J's too young; that's a pity. Aunt Irma could easily get married, of course; she could have been married twenty times over already. But she's so choosy. Can't make up her mind. So who does that leave?

Mother! That left Mother!

Pure logic had led Sue to the conclusion that Mother must get married, but she decided she couldn't wait for Mother to find a husband for herself. Anyway, Mother might pick the wrong man. Sue would look for a good husband for her. Someone handsome, clever, kind and amusing. And then life would be bound to improve for everyone!

Sue walked away from the window and sat down on the

chaise longue. As there was no one else in the room, she could put up her feet on the chaise longue, shoes and all. Aunt Irma's ballpoint pen was lying on the coffee table. Sue took a crumpled piece of paper out of her jeans pocket; it contained the maths homework she'd copied down yesterday from Helga Schubert. Sue wrote on the other side of the paper, which was blank:

MEN

Then she wrote down the names of all the men she knew who might do for Mother.

First she put 'Father'. She crossed that out straight away. That was no good; Mother had obviously had enough of *him*. She said so almost every day: to her friends on the phone, or to Aunt Irma. Sue had heard it over and over again.

Sue went on writing. In the end she had thirty-six names. Well, only thirty-three really, because 'man in check coat at bus stop' and 'fair-haired man in dairy' and 'man with dog called Kay' don't really count as names. Sue crossed those three out.

She crossed out Emmerich Hobelzahn as well. He might be a confectioner and quite nice really, but Sue didn't think she wanted Mother to marry him. Rather regretfully, she crossed out Karl Bunsenbichler and Anton Schimann. One squinted and the other limped, and Sue had once heard Mother say it must be difficult to love a man with a physical handicap.

That left thirty men. Sue crossed out five because she wasn't sure if they liked children. She crossed out seven more because they didn't have cars. And another three because their cars were so old. Another five went because Sue could see they were not really the right age for Mother: two of them were under twenty and the other three over seventy.

Then there was Mr Hameier, who was nice, and a good

39

piano teacher, but J didn't like him, so *he* wouldn't do. You had to think of your sister's feelings. Mr Broselmeier wasn't amusing enough. Mr Steininger wasn't clever enough; Sue was sure he wouldn't be much good at her maths homework. Leo Lindner, the vet, had a mother, a grandmother and three great-aunts; he went out for a walk with them every Sunday. Sue crossed him out, heavily. Dr Erich Meier-Traun-Forchtinger was very handsome and had a Mercedes 300, but he was terribly stand-offish.

'No good reaching for the stars,' muttered Sue, in a voice very like Aunt Alice's.

Carlo Brauner, who was Aunt Alice's godson, sat next to Mother when they went to the opera. He was always talking about music, and he said every child ought to learn a musical instrument, especially girls. No good. Mr Berger would have to go too, because he lisped when he talked. Mr Havranek stank of eau de Cologne.

In the end, Sue's short-list ran: First, Dr Alexander Hieberger, about forty, dental surgeon, lives three houses up the road, has two Hungarian shepherd dogs, one American car, what looks like a duelling scar on his face. Second, Dr Johannes Salamander, thirty-six, German teacher at Sue's school. Sue thought he had all the right qualities, physical and mental. He was her favourite.

Suddenly she felt more cheerful. She saw a glimmer of hope on the horizon, and the name of the glimmer was Dr Salamander. He was called Fiery Salamander at school, because he had red hair and because salamanders are supposed to be lizards who live in fire. Sue liked red hair and she liked Dr Salamander.

Sue began imagining family life with Fiery Salamander. Perhaps he and Mother would have children. Triplets! Triplets would be really exciting, especially red-headed triplets! Sue would take them out for walks, and everyone would stop and look into the special triplet pram and coo over the little Fiery Salamander babies.

And Fiery Salamander would mark all her compositions at school 'A'. And the other teachers would give her good marks too, because she was their colleague's stepdaughter. And Mother would wear a long, deep turquoise dress for the wedding. It would go with Dr Salamander's red hair.

Then Sue remembered that her parents weren't divorced yet, they were still married. Being married is a bit of a drawback when it comes to planning a wedding. Sue decided, however, that this could be fixed quite easily. Once Mother and Dr Salamander had agreed to marry, Father wouldn't be difficult. Well, it couldn't make much difference to a man who only wanted to keep Philip the cat. Or could it? Sue wasn't sure. There were so many different ways to think of Father. You could think how amusing and clever and nice and kind and handsome and cheerful he was. Or you could think how peculiar and mean and stubborn and pigheaded he was. There didn't seem to be anything in between those two ways of thinking about Father.

He had rung up once or twice and asked if Sue would like to come and see him. Or if he should fetch her and take her to the cinema or the park or the theatre. Mother had said she didn't mind; she explained she wasn't going to come between the children and their father. But Sue always refused, though part of her wanted to see Father.

Sue sighed and stood up, brushing the dirt from her shoes off the chaise longue, not that there was much of it. She put the list of men into her jeans pocket. She put Aunt Irma's ballpoint pen in her pocket too, because it wrote so well.

Sue went into the room she shared with J. It was a beastly room, a Chamber of Horrors. Every time Sue

41

opened the door she fairly stiffened at the sight of so many nasty things all in one room together.

But today she didn't mind the room so much. Sue was sure Fiery Salamander had a much nicer house, and she'd have a nice comfortable room there.

Sue sat down on the bed where she had to sleep at night. It was so high her toes could scarcely touch the ground. It had a velvet bedspread the colour of spinach, with red roses embroidered on it. If Sue rocked sideways on the bed it squeaked, and if she rocked backwards and forwards it groaned. Like Great-aunt Alice. If Great-aunt Alice had been dead, Sue would have believed her ghost lived under that mattress. Sue tried making up a poem:

Under the mattress of my bed
lies my great-aunt's ghost, who is dead,
and I am sitting on her ghostly chest.
If I could squash it flat that would be best.

Oh dear, thought Sue. No good at all. I can't even make up poetry these days.

J was lying on her bed, which was even higher than Sue's, and had flowered pleated curtains with little bows at either end. J was reading a thriller. J spent all her spare time reading thrillers.

Sue would have liked to tell J her plan about Fiery Salamander, and how there was a good chance they'd soon be out of Grandmother's house, but she realized it was no good. J had recently become a man-hater. J thought poorly of men in general. She had even thrown away any of her records where women were singing love songs about men. So Sue confined herself to saying, mysteriously, 'Ah, well, all things come to an end.' Naturally J did not catch her drift.

Sue lay down on the bed and shut her eyes. She thought: I should really be doing my homework. But she had more important things to think about. She had to decide how to bring Mother and Fiery Salamander together.

It wasn't all that easy. School was one place and home—or this house, which they had to call home—was another. Fiery Salamander was at school, and Mother was at home, and they didn't meet. It was all complicated by the fact that Sue had not been getting on too well with either Mother or Dr Salamander at the moment. Mother was annoyed with Sue for not being polite enough to Grandmother, and Dr Salamander was annoyed with her because of the way she didn't do her homework.

Indeed, the very next day he told her in school, 'Susanna, you know your work isn't very satisfactory. If you can't do better I'll have to ask your mother to come and see me.'

'Oh, yes! Please do!' cried Sue eagerly. 'Oh, thank you!'

And then Dr Salamander said she was being impertinent! However, Sue forgave him. One ought to be magnanimous.

Sue was very magnanimous. She had forgiven lots of teachers for finding her work unsatisfactory. The teachers here at secondary school were very odd. They wanted to know such funny things. In arithmetic, for instance, which they called mathematics here. Sue couldn't seem to get it. There was the set theory, for instance. You were supposed to know what $(M1 - M2)(M1 + M2)$ meant. To Sue's surprise, most of the children did seem to know.

When you don't understand something at school, of course you can always ask the teacher to explain. But Sue didn't even understand enough to ask the right questions. She would have had to get up in a maths lesson and say, 'Please, sir, I don't understand any of it at all. Would you mind going right back to the beginning?' And who'd dare say a thing like that?

Sue did try to do some maths with her sister, but that usually led to a quarrel. J would say Sue was going to get thrown out of the school at this rate, she was a hopeless case and a complete idiot. Which was probably true, because Sue had learnt that three plus two make five. So how could the union of two with three suddenly come out as three? Sue would shout desperately at J, 'For goodness' sake, two sausages and three sausages on my plate make five sausages. Anyone can see that!'

J shouted back that that was right with sausages, but wrong with the set theory. Then J did Sue's maths homework for her, and Sue copied it into her exercise book.

'Now do you understand?' J asked. Sue nodded and assured her that she did, though it was not true. She might have been copying out Chinese calligraphy, for all the sense the mathematical symbols made to her.

There was quite a lot Sue disliked about her new school. She was over in Benny's kitchen one day, soon after she'd decided Mother ought to marry Dr Salamander, moaning about Miss Zahn the biology teacher. 'She's got a nerve, she really has!' said Sue indignantly.

'How do you mean?' asked Benny.

Sue explained. 'Twice a week she comes and talks to us and draws things on the board. And she said we were only to make notes about the things we thought really import-ant. She definitely said that.'

'Well?' said Benny. 'So what's the matter?'

'She was cross with me,' said Sue.

Benny, who was good at school work, still didn't understand. '*Why* was she cross with you?'

'Because I hadn't made any notes,' said Sue.

'What, none at all?' Benny stared at her.

'Well,' Sue muttered, 'I did put a heading on the first

page of my exercise book. It says MAN. I wrote it in my best writing, too, and I underlined it in red.' And Sue added, 'Honestly, Benny, it isn't that I'm lazy. She *didn't* say anything I thought really important. I kept on waiting for the important bit, and it didn't come.'

Benny shook his head. 'Sue, they *will* throw you out of that school if you go on like this,' he said.

That evening, lying in her high bed, the lamp with the mauve-beaded shade on beside her, Sue thought: It's high time I got Fiery Salamander into this family. If I don't I might get thrown out of school, just like J and Benny say.

Right, thought Sue, what have I done so far? Not much, really. I keep telling Mother how nice Dr Salamander is, but she doesn't really seem to notice. All she says is, 'Well, I'm glad you get on so well with your German teacher, dear. Mind you work hard for him!'

'No, it's not good enough,' muttered Sue, switching off the lamp, mauve beads and all.

5

Time went by. Nothing awful happened; nothing very nice happened either.

J kept doing her homework and learning Latin vocabulary and watching television and reading thrillers.

Aunt Irma had 'flu and stayed in bed, resting, for two weeks.

Great-aunt Alice cleaned and dusted and straightened things and improved the shining hour with proverbs and complained that no one ever told her anything.

Mother spent all day at the Soho Lady, doing overtime in the evenings, because at this time of year all the customers were buying winter coats and dresses.

Grandmother was more like a sergeant-major than ever. Business was not too good at the shop, because of Aunt Irma being ill. As Grandmother did not have deep blue eyes or blonde hair, let alone dimples, she was not so good as persuading gentlemen to buy butter churns and milking stools, and if Grandmother went a couple of days without selling anything much she became quite unbearable.

But at last something did happen.

Sue and J had their birthdays. Sue's birthday was really October 20th and J's was October 24th, but Aunt Alice decided they should have a joint birthday on the 22nd. She said two birthday cakes so close together would be bad for the digestion.

The birthday cake Aunt Alice made looked lovely, but

unfortunately she had put a lot of rum in the cream filling, and Sue hated the taste of rum. Aunt Alice's feelings were hurt. She said the recipe for the cake came from the Austrian imperial court, and if it had been good enough for the Emperor of Austria's children it was good enough for Sue! Mother said Sue might at least have a taste. Sue refused to have a taste. Grandmother said the children of today ought to have known what wartime was like, then the children of today would be able to appreciate a good cake. The only person who was happy was J, who liked the taste of rum, and was embarking on her fourth slice of cake while this argument was in progress. In fact Sue was hungry all day on the 22nd, because she didn't like the roast venison they had for dinner either.

'Hunger is the best sauce,' Aunt Alice told her, and Sue realized, with a kind of grim satisfaction, that even birthdays were horrible in the Buchinger household.

Sue had a lot of presents, of course, and some of them were quite useful, though she didn't know what to do with the autograph book with pastel-coloured pages. You weren't supposed to write your own poetry in it, you were supposed to get your girl friends to put verses in it. Sue supposed she was meant to give it to someone like Annie and let her scribble:

Roses are red,
Violets are blue,
Sugar is sweet
And so are you!

Or:

Patience is a virtue
Virtue is a grace,
Grace was a little girl
Who wouldn't wash her face.

47

And then Annie would sign it 'From your affectionate friend Annie. Forget me not.'

As it happened, Sue and Annie couldn't stand each other. Sue's only friends were Benny Meier, and Karl Novotny who was in her class at school. And she didn't need to ask them to write in her album; she'd never forget them anyway, not if she lived to be a hundred.

The twelve balls of bright pink wool Grandmother gave Sue for her birthday weren't very exciting either.

And she didn't actually need that little bottle of lily-of-the-valley scent, but she thought Aunt Irma meant well.

J gave Sue a lovely penknife with four blades.

Mother gave her a new long-length coat with fox fur round the hem. And a crinkly-look patent leather brief-case for school. And a leather skirt, and some new felt pens. They were all very nice; the only trouble was that apparently Benny Meier didn't like long-length coats.

Two parcels came from Father. Sue's contained a splendid camera, exactly what she wanted. And Father had bought J a Russian cap, exactly what *she* wanted. And best of all, Sue's parcel came on October 20th and J's on October 24th. Not on the 22nd, the way they did things in this house.

Father had put a letter in with the camera. He wrote to say he was missing Sue a lot, and he wished she'd visit him some time; if she didn't want to come to the apartment, would she like to meet him at his office? (Sue had always loved going to Father's office.)

Sue rang Father up; Mother had told her to ring and thank him for the birthday present. And Father invited her out again. 'Yes, please,' Sue said over the phone. 'I'd like to come.'

Father said he'd pick Sue up from school tomorrow and they'd go and have lunch in a restaurant. Sue wasn't quite sure if she would still want to go next day.

But next day, after school, Father was waiting there outside the school gates, and either Sue had entirely forgotten what he looked like, or he had changed a lot. He was looking very handsome and very smart. It wasn't only Sue who thought so; girls from the older classes looked admiringly at Father as they passed him.

'Hey, great!' said Sue.

'What is?' asked Father.

'You!' said Sue.

'Well, thanks!' said Father. They went to the car.

'I borrowed Jonny's old banger in your honour,' said Father. (Jonny was Father's brother, and his 'old banger' was an Alfa Romeo.)

It felt good, getting into a snow-white Alfa Romeo, with the whole class gawping at you. Especially with someone like Father holding the door open while you got in. Father's hair had grown. It curled over his shirt collar, black and glossy. His shirt collar itself was twice as high as it used to be. And Father had a lilac silk tie, and a black leather suit.

'How about taking Jonny to lunch with us?' asked Father. 'He's dying to see you again.'

Sue nodded.

'What sort of restaurant would you like?' asked Father.

Sue didn't know.

'We could go to an Indian restaurant, or a Chinese one, or a Serbian or Italian or Greek or English restaurant, or just an ordinary Viennese one.'

Sue didn't want to go to an ordinary Viennese restaurant. 'What's the poshest kind of restaurant?' she asked.

'French.'

'Then let's go to a French restaurant,' Sue decided.

Then she began wondering if she was posh enough herself for a French restaurant. Her fingernails were rather dirty, there was a ladder in her tights and a spot on her skirt, and the skirt itself was creased from being sat in. But Father said really classy people didn't bother about little things like that.

It was nice sitting beside Father in the car; it was such a lovely car and Father drove so well. When Mother drove you mustn't talk to her. Mother kept staring at the road, and she clung tight to the steering wheel and said rude things about the people in other cars. But Father drove as casually as other people walk. He didn't have to keep looking at the road; when he said something to Sue he glanced at her. Outside the building where Father and Uncle Jonny had their office, Father drove once forward, once back, and there he was neatly parked in a tiny little space. It would have taken Mother at least ten mano-euvres to get into that space, and she'd have had to wind down the window, and get Sue and J and three passers-by to help guide her in.

Father had a new notice outside the building where his office was. It said K & K Advertising, in bright orange on bright green. (The old notice had said *Kaufmann Bros., Advertising Agents,* but Father said the old notice wasn't very trendy.)

Uncle Jonny was waiting upstairs in the office. He was younger than Father. Sue thought he looked marvellous. He had fair shoulder-length hair, velvet trousers, desert boots, and a white silk shirt with embroidery on it. And a long, thick silver chain round his neck with a glass eye hanging from it. A genuine glass eye.

'Got it from a firm that makes them,' said Uncle Jonny. And he gave Sue the silver chain with the glass eye, because, he said, she was his favourite niece. Sue put the chain round her neck. 'Do you think I could wear it to school?' she asked.

Uncle Jonny and Father didn't know, but Uncle Jonny said in her place he'd wear it to school. If there'd been such things around in his young days, he said, he'd have worn a glass eye round his neck to school like a shot. Father said he was a liar, he'd always been a coward, and he'd never have ventured inside the school gates with a glass eye round his neck. Uncle Jonny said that was an insult, and he demanded satisfaction.

'A duel! Sir, I insist upon a duel!' he shouted at Father.

Sue handed Father and Uncle Jonny two rulers. 'Ready, gentlemen?' she asked. 'Go!'

Father and Uncle Jonny had a tremendous duel with the two rulers, until Father forced Uncle Jonny right up against the cloakroom door.

Then the phone rang, and they let Sue pick it up and say, 'Sorry, this is the Dogs' and Cats' Swimming Baths and Rest Home.' And then, 'Oh, that's all right, sir, anyone can get a wrong number. What a shame! You wanted Kaufmann and Kaufmann? Oh, I think they've gone to Alaska. Yes, to advertise polar bears. Now do remember, sir, if you ever turn into a dog, my establishment is at your disposal any time!'

Father and Uncle Jonny were close to the phone, barking like mad, and just at this moment Sue really couldn't understand why she had not wanted to see Father before.

A little later Uncle Jonny asked, 'Well, and how are you, Sue?'

'Just now,' said Sue, 'I feel like a dried-up oasis in a sudden shower of rain!'

'Now don't you start going poetic on us, love,' said Father.

Then the three of them went to a French restaurant. It was a very French restaurant indeed. Everything was red, white and blue: the tablecloths, the menus, the napkins, the coat stand. Anything not red, white and blue was made of brass or marble.

Father and Uncle Jonny ordered something which sounded like *booee-a-base*. Sue thought that sounded nice, but when she discovered it was made of fish she decided not to have it. She had a hot patty called *Louis XIV* instead. After that, they all three had something called a *Chatoh-breeah*. The waiter didn't just bring three separate plates, each with a piece of meat on it: it was much more exciting that that. He wheeled a little trolley with a board and a long, sharp knife on it up to their table. Then two other waiters came along wheeling a smaller trolley, which held the silver dish containing the *Chatoh-breeah*. Then the head waiter himself came up, transferred the meat from the silver dish to the board and carved it with the long, sharp knife. He carved it slowly, thoughtfully and with obvious enjoyment.

'That man has surgeon's hands,' whispered Father, winking at Sue. While the head waiter was carving the meat, the others were serving peas, baby carrots, asparagus and tiny cobs of sweet corn. Then the first waiter came up with yet another trolley, full of bottles of different sauces and seasonings. Then the wine waiter came and opened a bottle of wine for Father and Uncle Jonny. He twisted and turned the bottle like a conjuror at the circus saying, 'Look, gentlemen, no tricks, no false bottom!' Father and Uncle Jonny looked admiringly at the bottle. So did Sue.

'*Chatoh-nerf-dew-pup,*' murmured Father.

'The 'forty-seven,' whispered the wine waiter.

Uncle Jonny nodded with satisfaction.

Later Sue had a *Parfay oh caffay*, but it was only a coffee ice really. Father ate some cheese with a completely unpronounceable name.

Finally the head waiter came with the bill, wrapped in a napkin on a golden salver. Father raised the napkin a little so that he could see the figures at the bottom of the bill.

Then he casually took a note out of his pocket. A very big note indeed. He pushed it casually under the napkin, and just as casually the head waiter picked up the salver with the napkin. A little later he put the salver back on the table. Father's change was lying under the napkin. Sue might not be very good at the set theory, but she could do simple subtraction all right. She counted the change, subtracted it from the big note, and caught her breath in amazement. Father had paid as much for that meal as he used to give Mother for a whole week's housekeeping! And he was always telling Mother she had no idea how to manage money!

'Goodness, Father, you *have* changed!' said Sue.

Father didn't know what Sue meant, but Uncle Jonny did. He grinned and gave a chuckle. 'That's my doing, love. He's enjoying life these days. Not a staid old family man any more, eh? Someone to be proud of, Sue, dear!'

Sue nodded, but without much enthusiasm. She was remembering the Dior perfume at the airport. However, she did not have long to think about it before another surprise was sprung on her. The head waiter was saying goodbye to Father, hoping to see him again soon, and then he looked at Sue and said, 'Why, your little girl there is the very image of her big sister!'

'What?' said Sue.

'The image of your big sister, miss!' the head waiter repeated. 'Same blue eyes, same pretty little nose!'

Sue wanted to ask the head waiter how on earth he knew J. But then a lady walked past them, stopped, and stared in horror at Sue's neck, where the glass eye was dangling. Father nodded to the lady and said, in confidential tones, 'Property of our grandmother. We're taking it out for a walk. She's a cripple, poor old lady, and that eye of hers never gets any fresh air.'

The lady shook her head crossly. But then she took a

closer look at Father. Father gave her a charming smile, and the lady smiled back.

Later, sitting between Father and Uncle Jonny in the car—there was room for three in the front seat of the Alfa Romeo—Sue asked, 'How come the head waiter has met J?'

Uncle Jonny laughed. 'Met her, love?' he said. 'He's devoted to her! Says she's as tender as a nice *entrecôte* steak, as sparkling as champagne, as sweet as a chocolate éclair, as piquant as *salade niçoise* . . . .'

'And smells as good as a cheese soufflé!' Father finished.

Sue was no expert on cheese soufflés or éclairs or entrecôte steaks, but she knew her sister pretty well. She fairly ground her teeth with rage. Sue only ever ground her teeth if she was really furious.

Father was observant. He was just overtaking another car, but he noticed Sue grinding her teeth.

'Are you angry?' he asked, surprised.

'Not with you,' spat Sue.

'Nor me, I hope?' asked Uncle Jonny.

'No; J!' said Sue.

'Oh, come on, don't be silly!' Father laughed. 'When the head waiter knows you as well as J, he'll say you're as delicious as *ris de veau à la financière!*'

Sue nodded and smiled. She pretended not to be angry any more, but she was. And Father wasn't all that clever if he really thought it was those silly compliments about French food that annoyed her.

Sisters! thought Sue. Making out she hated all men. Saying how horrible they were. Saying she didn't want anything to do with Father. The way she went on about him in Yugoslavia! And then going out regularly with Father and Uncle Jonny—driving in fast cars and eating

French food! She probably goes out every Thursday and Friday when she says she's doing Latin homework with Erna. My sister is a *cow!*

Sue blew her nose furiously into a handkerchief Uncle Jonny had lent her, and mumbled into it, 'Cheese soufflé, is she? Cheesed off, that's me!'

Then Sue forgot to be furious, because she realized Father was driving out to the nice farm in the Vienna woods. The farmer had two dogs, four cows, and so many cats you couldn't count them. While they were there Sue played with the cats. One of them looked just like Philip. As she was stroking the cat's tummy for him, Father and Uncle Jonny talked business. They were discussing some manufacturer who made office furniture, and had produced ten thousand executive chairs, trade name Boss. And now no one wanted to buy the chairs, so the office furniture manufacturer, on the verge of ruin, had gone to K & K Advertising and given Father the job of publicizing his Boss executive chairs.

'We can have a picture of the Boss chair on the cover of the furniture brochure,' Father was saying. 'And have one in any of the pictures showing desks.'

'It could go in the shaver ad, too,' said Uncle Jonny. 'Suppose we have the man with the close, clean shave sitting in a Boss chair?'

'You think we could seat the TV breakfast cereal baby on that wretched Boss chair too?' asked Father.

Uncle Jonny nodded, obviously pleased. Sue couldn't quite make it out. She asked why they wanted to put a chair no one liked in their advertising pictures.

'Clear as mud, Sue,' Father explained. 'We want people to see so much of that chair they end of thinking if they keep on seeing it so often, it must be something marvellous.'

'It gets into their subconscious, see?' said Uncle Jonny.

'Subliminal advertising.'

And he poked Sue in the tummy with his forefinger. This convinced Sue that the subconscious was situated somewhere in one's tummy, not that that mattered. The important thing was for Sue to get the hang of advertising methods, because she intended to use them.

I must advertise, Sue told herself. Advertisement, that's it! Oh, if only I'd known all this a month ago we'd have hooked Fiery Salamander by now!

There was trouble when Sue got home. Mother and Grandmother said she was not to wear the glass eye. 'A disgusting thing like that, round a young girl's neck!' said Aunt Alice. 'I never saw anything so revolting!'

Sue didn't want to let the glass eye go, but Mother simply took the chain off her neck and said it would be sent back to Uncle Jonny, and she was not letting anyone make her children entirely crazy, particularly not that frivolous young man. Sue ground her teeth with rage again, and then remembered how and why she had been so angry earlier that afternoon. She went into the Chamber of Horrors, made J stop reading her thriller and told her exactly what she thought of her, meeting Father in secret. J didn't seem to mind.

'Look, baby sister, I don't have to account to you for everything I do,' she said.

'But you ought to have told Mother,' Sue said, virtuously. (It was amazing how quickly Sue could become virtuous.)

'Oh, I ought, ought I?' shouted J. 'It's not *my* fault they've separated! I've a right to see my father whenever I like, not just when Mother says. I'm not a piece of furniture to be carted round and plonked down in a new house somewhere!'

'That wasn't the way you talked before!' Sue shouted

back.

'Well, people can change their minds, can't they?' said J. 'I realized Father's nice, that's all. Mother's nice too, only they don't suit each other.'

'But that's nonsense!' said Sue. 'Two nice people would be bound to suit each other.'

J didn't answer, she just laughed.

'Anyway, Mother and Father got married, right?' Sue went on. 'So why didn't they notice they didn't suit each other then? Look, if they hadn't suited each other they wouldn't have got married at all, would they?'

'Oh, for goodness' sake, how ignorant can you get?' said J. 'They didn't know each other properly before they got married, that's all.'

'How silly can *you* get?' snapped Sue. 'They'd known each other for three years! Mother told me.'

'There are different ways of knowing someone,' J told her sister. 'You think Father knew Mother would be going round the house with her hair in rollers ten years later? You think he knew she'd be getting fat, and so she'd be jealous of thin women? And she'd always be having headaches and migraines? And Uncle Jonny would get on her nerves? How could he have known that?'

Sue shook her head, sadly.

J went on, 'And how could Mother know Father would take against her family? And like going out with his friends better than going out with her? And start up the K & K Advertising business, instead of staying in that big factory's publicity department and maybe getting to be managing director some day? How could she have known that?'

Sue did not have any answers. Indeed, she had not even realized that rollers and Uncle Jonny and K & K Advertising and headaches were so important. But she was sticking to her guns. 'Do listen, J,' she said. 'All right, so

57

Mother's not as nice as she used to be, and nor is Father. But I love them both, so they can't be all that horrible! And if I'm fond of them both, they must be able to be fond of each other. Mustn't they?'

J sighed.

Sue decided not to pursue the subject any further for the moment. Anyway, getting out of their present situation was what mattered. Dr Salamander was what mattered! (A few days ago Karl at school had told Sue Dr Salamander had a house in a nice residential area, with a garden, and a cat.)

Sue fished her school briefcase out from under the bed, turned out the entire contents on top of the bed and sorted through them until her German composition book rose to the surface of the heap.

'How doth the little busy bee . . .' said J, sarcastically.

'Better late than never,' Sue told her. (A few weeks in the same house as Aunt Alice had taught them any amount of proverbs.)

As it happened, Sue had not intended to do her homework at all. She had planned to say at school that she was very sorry, but she'd left her composition at home. However, advertising was all-important. She opened the exercise book and sat down at the little table. (There was no big table in the room.) She stuck her thumb in her mouth and thought. She was supposed to be writing a short composition called 'A Walk in the Woods'. Sue took the top off her fountain pen and wrote:

'A Walk in the Woods'   *16th November*
Yesterday I went to the woods with my mother. My mother is very beautiful and very nice. She has fair hair and she is just plump enough to be the right size. She has lovely white teeth with hardly any fillings, the dentist says that is unusual at her age. Also my mother

is very clever and very kind. She has a very important job in a shop selling ladies' clothes. It was beautiful in the woods.

'There,' said Sue. 'That'll do for a start.'

'Want me to check it for mistakes?' asked J.

Sue put the exercise book back in her case.

'No thanks,' she said. 'There aren't any.' Then she had another idea. She took a clean sheet of blotting paper out of the drawer in the table and drew a beautiful lady on it in red felt pen. With curly hair, pointed breasts and a tiny waist. The curly hair and pointed breasts took up a lot of space, so the lady's legs had to be very short.

Sue held up the picture. 'Who's that?' she asked.

J looked. 'The ugly old caretaker at the Irmingers' villa,' she said at once.

'Oh, don't be silly!' snapped Sue. 'It's Mother!'

'Well, don't show it to her, that's all!' J giggled. 'She's rather sensitive about her appearance.'

Sue thought J was always finding fault. It wasn't a bad picture at all. Especially the curls; they were very lifelike. And Mother's legs weren't particularly long in real life.

Sue wrote MOTHER in block capitals under the picture, and slipped it inside her German book. She felt she could sleep soundly now.

6

At school next day, Dr Salamander asked for volunteers
to read their compositions about a walk in the woods. Sue
put her hand up. Dr Salamander was surprised: Sue never
usually volunteered. So he picked her. When she had
finished reading her composition the whole class was in
fits of laughter.

'It's rude to laugh at people!' Dr Salamander told them.
That was nice of him. Sue flashed him a smile.

'However, I'm sorry, Sue,' said Dr Salamander, 'but I
can't give you a very good mark for that composition.
You didn't write about a walk in the woods, you wrote
about your delightful mother.'

Sue beamed at Dr Salamander. She thought: He said
'delightful mother'. She sat down, perfectly happy.

After this Sue never forgot to do her homework for Dr
Salamander; she even did extra. If he told them to make
up ten sentences she made up twenty. If he told them to
write one page about something Sue wrote two.

Sue produced some most impressive exercises in gram-
mar and syntax. When asked to give examples of words
ending in -ing, -ation, -ate, -ish, -hood, -ism, Sue wrote:
mothering, motheration, motherate, motherish, mother-
hood, motherism. And when making adjectives ending
-ful from nouns, Sue wrote: Hate—hateful; Beauty—
beautiful; Tear—tearful, and added Mother—motherful.

Fiery Salamander began looking at Sue very hard and

very thoughtfully during lessons. Sue was pleased to see that his gaze sometimes rested on her for ages.

One day she was sitting at home, doing her homework, which was a list of verbs to be used both in the active and the passive. She wrote:

My beautiful mother collects.
My nice mother breaks.
My brave mother holds.
My clever mother finds.
My beautiful mother is collected.
My nice mother is broken.
My brave mother is held.

At this point J looked over her shoulder. J was horrified. 'Are you trying to annoy Dr Salamander or something?' she asked.

'Certainly not,' said Sue, finishing: My clever mother is found.

Dr Salamander was very kind to Sue. He always looked at her book first. He read her work slowly and carefully, and sometimes he patted Sue's head. That was a great triumph. But Sue still felt things were moving too slowly.

That phrase Uncle Jonny had used about subliminal advertising came back to her, and on her next visit to Father—Sue visited Father once a week now—she asked him what it was. Father explained, but either he explained subliminal advertising badly, or Sue didn't understand. Or maybe she just wasn't listening hard enough, because she was stroking Philip the cat. Anyway, Sue formed her own rather individual ideas of subliminal advertising, and she put them into practice next time Dr Salamander gave them dictation.

He opened a book of fairy tales. 'Snow White and the Seven Dwarves,' he dictated.

Sue wrote down: 'Snow Mother and the Seven Mothers.' And she went on: 'Once upon a mother in the middle of mother, when mothers were falling from the sky like mothers, a mother sat mothering at her mother, which had a frame of black mother. And as she mothered and looked out at the mother, she pricked her finger with the mother, and three drops of mother fell on the mother. The red mothers looked so motherly that the mother thought to herself, "Oh, if only I had a mother as white as mother, as red as mother and as black as mother!"'

Sue went on like this for two more pages. Finally she wrote 'Mother, Mother, Mother' right across the bottom of the dictation, and gave her book in. She smiled brilliantly at Fiery Salamander and went back to her place.

Sue felt very happy for the last two lessons of the day. She knew she had done well. 'Fortune favours the bold,' Aunt Alice used to say, and Sue was sure Fortune would favour her.

Today being Thursday, Sue particularly disliked going home. Thursday was plum dumpling day. Great-aunt Alice made plum dumplings every Thursday, just as she had done for the last forty years, even if Christmas or Grandmother's birthday happened to fall on a Thursday, and she said she was not going to alter her ways just for Sue. Sue did not like plum dumplings; in fact, she hated them. Aunt Alice took no notice. Every Thursday lunch time she put a huge plateful of plum dumplings in front of Sue. Sue couldn't even stand the smell of them; she had to turn her head aside so as not to feel ill.

'Hunger is the best sauce!' Aunt Alice would say. And she pointed out that there were four eggs in the dumpling dough, and the breadcrumbs were fried in butter, and the plum sauce was home-made.

Sue still could not eat the dumplings. Today she

pushed the plate away and stood up.

'Well, you're not getting anything else!' said Aunt Alice. 'However hungry you may feel,' she added, as Sue went to the door.

Sue opened the kitchen door, but before closing it behind her she said, 'I'm having lunch with Father tomorrow, so if I don't have anything to eat today I can eat twice as much Peking duck tomorrow.'

Aunt Alice looked really shocked. 'Peking duck!' she muttered. 'I always said Fred spoilt those children. Peking duck!' She flung the kitchen door open and screeched after Sue, 'Well, *I'm* not nursing you if that foreign muck gives you indigestion!' Then she said, 'Somebody called Dr Iguana rang up.'

'What?' Sue stopped dead.

'Iguana,' repeated Aunt Alice. 'He said he was your German teacher.'

'Salamander, Salamander!' cried Sue, delighted. 'Fiery Salamander!'

She hopped from one foot to the other; she was so pleased she almost hugged Aunt Alice, but that would have been overdoing it, and she drew back at the last moment. However, she forgave Aunt Alice for the plum dumplings.

Then she asked for more precise information. First Aunt Alice said, as usual, that she didn't know anything about it because no one ever told her anything. However, then it turned out that she knew quite a lot.

'This Dr Iguana rang up to speak to Caroline. I told him she wouldn't be in till evening. He said it was very urgent, so I gave him her number at the Soho Lady.'

'What else? Is that all?' asked Sue.

'What else? Oh, Caroline rang me to say she'd be late home this evening because she's going to meet this Iguana person.'

'It worked!' cried Sue. 'It worked!'

And she danced into the Chamber of Horrors.

Aunt Alice could think of no suitable proverb to describe Sue's peculiar behaviour. But as she always had to produce some kind of proverbial saying, she remarked darkly, 'Don't count your chickens before they're hatched.'

The old lady had no idea how right she was.

Sue spent all afternoon picturing the meeting of Fiery Salamander and Caroline Kaufmann. Perhaps Fiery Salamander would say, 'Dear lady, I can no longer live without you!' No, thought Sue, he wouldn't say that. More likely: 'Mrs Kaufmann, I hardly know how to account for it, but something in my subconscious tells me I must get to know you!'

Sue started waiting for Mother at seven o'clock. She waited outside the front door, where she could not annoy Aunt Alice, because Aunt Alice didn't see her. She was cleaning out the kitchen cupboard where the jam jars were kept, muttering, 'A place for everything and everything in its place.'

Grandmother and Aunt Irma came home, and told Sue to go indoors.

J came home from visiting Father, and told Sue she'd catch cold.

Benny shouted over the fence, 'Coming over, Sue?'

Sue shook her head.

'Are you practising sentry duty, or did the old girl send you out for a punishment?' asked Benny.

'I'm expecting a change of fortune any minute!' Sue called back. Benny went back to his own house, so as not to disturb her.

And at last Mother came home. She looked very pale.

Sue was surprised to find that happiness could make you so pale. Mother hugged Sue, whispering, 'Oh, my poor darling!'

It was like something out of a film again, only not a film with wedding bells and a happy ending, a film where someone is going to die. Sue thought this odd. Mother did tend to be emotional, but she never acted as if she were in quite the wrong sort of film. Sue freed herself from Mother's embrace and asked, 'What's the matter?'

Mother began crying and saying she had been neglecting Sue, leaving her to deal with her problems all alone, but she would try to make up for it now.

Sue helped Mother, who seemed to be feeling weak, into the house and up to her bedroom. It was some time before she could make out just why Mother was so upset and tearful, but when Sue did realize why, her rage knew no bounds. Her teeth ground like gravel crunching underfoot.

Fiery Salamander had told Mother that Sue was going nuts! At least, he said she was severely mentally disturbed; she had a neurosis, or worse. And to prove it he'd shown Sue's mother her exercise book, and he said if something was not done for Sue soon, he feared for her sanity!

Sue had great powers of self-control. She was furious, and her hopes had been shattered, but she could still think calmly and clearly about the best way to act.

She decided she would pretend not to know anything about it. 'But Mother, I did hear right!' she said. 'He really did dictate "Snow Mother and the Seven Mothers"!'

'Yes, yes, dear, don't get upset,' whispered Mother, stroking Sue's head. 'We'll soon make it better.'

'Can I go and play with Benny?' Sue asked. She did not care for this conversation a bit; she was anxious to get away from Mother.

'Yes, yes, my chicken,' whispered Mother. 'Off you go,

but don't be too long.'

Sue tiptoed quietly out of the house, with Mother looking soulfully after her. When Sue was round the corner she began to run. She galloped up the fence, scrambled over into the Meiers' garden and rang their bell, loud and long.

That dreadful man Meier opened the door. 'House on fire?' he asked.

'My hopes have gone up in smoke, that's all,' said Sue. 'I want to talk to Benny about it.'

'You have my heartfelt sympathy,' said Mr Meier. Then Benny came along, and Mr Meier went away. He was a tactful person, and didn't want to disturb them.

Sue told Benny the whole story, ending up, 'Benny, did I make a mess of it?'

'I'll say you did! A complete and utter mess!' said Benny. Then he asked, 'Now what are you going to do?'

'Well, I've got Dr Hieberger in reserve,' Sue said. 'I could keep having toothache. Mother always goes to the dentist with me. If I have toothache every day Mother will be bound to get to know Dr Hieberger pretty well, shouldn't you think?'

Benny shook his head. 'For one thing, Dr Hieberger only treats fee-paying private patients, so your mother won't take you to him, and for another his receptionist wouldn't like it.'

'What's my toothache got to do with her?' asked Sue.

'She's married to Dr Hieberger,' said Benny, 'and they have two children.'

By now Sue was feeling really depressed. A desolate future lay ahead.

'Mind you, the advertising idea's not bad,' said Benny. 'But you need a new product, and a better-organized campaign.'

'What?'

'I mean you need a different man, and you'll have to set about it more sensibly.'

'But I can't think of any other men.'

'Sue, I don't want to push in where I'm not wanted,' said Benny. 'But have you considered my dad?'

'Benny.' Sue jumped up and flung her arms round Benny's neck. 'You're a genius! He'd be even better than Dr Salamander!'

'And we could both advertise,' said Benny.

'And then we'd be brother and sister!' cried Sue.

With Benny's help, Sue constructed a new and better future on the ruins of her hopes. They began planning their campaign at once, but they were disturbed in the middle of it by Mr Meier, who came into the room saying, 'Sorry to disturb you, but there's a female standing by the garden fence bawling herself hoarse.'

'That must be my dear, nice mother,' said Sue, giving Mr Meier a beaming smile.

'Wouldn't know one from the other,' muttered Mr Meier. 'Those Buchinger women are all alike.'

'My mother is the nicest, prettiest of them all!' fluted Sue.

'Very likely,' said Mr Meier. 'She was the fattest girl in the neighbourhood as a child, though. Always crying, too.'

'Oh, have you known my mother all that time?' asked Sue.

'Yes, we've always lived here,' said Mr Meier. 'So have the Buchingers.'

'Did you play with my mother when you were little?' asked Sue.

'Heaven forbid!' said Mr Meier.

'Don't you *like* my mother?' Sue looked pleadingly into Mr Meier's eyes. He hardly liked to say 'No', so he muttered, 'Why yes, of course.'

'Oh, good. That's all right, then,' said Sue, relieved. She went home, winking unobtrusively at Benny as she left, though apparently not unobtrusively enough, because Mr Meier asked if she had something in her eye. Sue said, 'No, but how *kind* of you to ask, Mr Meier.' And she went out of the house.

'Sounds as if she's going off her head too, like the rest of the family,' said Mr Meier to his son.

Sue ran to the fence, where Mother was waiting. Mother said it was high time Sue was in bed, and asked if she felt strong enough to climb the fence. Sue said she'd try. Sure enough, she was strong enough to climb the fence. Mother seemed pleased, and told Sue she needn't go to school next day, Mother was taking her to see a doctor at eleven.

Sue was not the sort of child who is silly enough to be afraid of doctors. She liked going to the surgery and saying 'Aah', having her chest listened to and her feet examined to see if they were flat, and afterwards the doctor always gave her three sheets of blotting paper with a printed heading saying, 'Excess stomach acid? Insufficient stomach acid? Take Patent Gastric Drops.'

But today Sue was to see a different kind of doctor: a psychiatrist. Because of writing 'Mother' all over her exercise book.

Sue lay in bed that morning, and didn't get up till J had gone to school, much to J's annoyance. 'What are you up to this time?' J asked.

'I'm not up to anything,' Sue said, keeping her eyes closed. 'I'm neurotic.'

'It's no good trying to make me believe you're nuts,' J said. 'I haven't the faintest idea why you kept writing "Mother" in your exercise book, but you're no more crazy than I am.'

'Perhaps you're crazy too,' said Sue.

'Idiot,' said J, going out of the room.

Sue lay there in bed thinking about her visit to the doctor. She thought: if I go on pretending to be stupid, he may prescribe special treatment. She didn't want treatment, and she didn't think the Kaufmann family's medical insurance would run to free psychiatric treatment anyway. It would be mean to make Mother pay for something she didn't need.

Aunt Alice brought Sue breakfast in bed, and without a single proverb either. Sue felt quite kindly towards Aunt Alice, until she saw that her breakfast was dry toast and camomile tea. She asked why, since it was her mind and not her digestion that was supposed to be ill, but Aunt Alice said something about *mens sana in corpore sano* and mind and body being one.

While she drank some of the camomile tea, Sue wondered what to say to the psychiatrist. Mother came and helped her get dressed. Sue had to wear her best dress, and Mother tied her hair back in a ponytail. She still hadn't decided what to tell the psychiatrist.

She had no time to think about it in the car, either. They had reached the doctor's consulting rooms before she managed to find a comfortable place to sit on the battered old car seat. I'll decide in the waiting room, before it's our turn, Sue thought. (All the doctors' waiting rooms she had ever been in were full of people.)

As it happened, there wasn't a single other person in the waiting room, and a very pretty receptionist took them in to the doctor. The doctor was young and good-looking, with a nice face and longish hair. He looked like Uncle Jonny or Father, and Sue didn't want to pretend she was stupid to him at all. He probably wouldn't believe me if I did, either, she thought. She said politely, 'Good morning.'

'Good morning,' said the doctor. Then he said Sue's mother had already spoken to him on the phone, and he had had a word with Dr Salamander, who had recommended Mother to come to him.

Mother started telling the doctor about Sue's home background, but he said that could wait, and asked Mother if she would mind leaving them alone. He and Sue would be some time, so why didn't she go and have a cup of coffee? Obviously Mother would rather have stayed in the room, but you have to do what a doctor says. She kissed Sue's cheek and said she didn't think she could swallow any coffee, she'd be in the waiting room.

That left Sue alone with the doctor. He asked if she would be kind enough to do a few tests. Yes, Sue said, she would be kind enough. She sat down in a nice red chair at a nice red table, and he gave her some half-finished pictures. Sue had to finish them.

Then he gave her some pictures to look at. They were all spots, blurred together, looking as if someone had shaken ink over a piece of paper and then folded it up to splodge the inkspots. Sue was supposed to say what she thought the inkspots looked alike. That was fun: one picture looked like the sea, and another looked like Philip the cat.

'And that's Aunt Alice,' she said, pointing at the biggest, blackest smudge of all.

Then the doctor gave her a piece of paper with a row of letters on it. Some of the letters were missing, and there were dots instead of them, so that it looked something like this:

ab.mn.bcm.a.cmn.bc.n

Sue was to decide which letters were supposed to go in which spaces. She could have done that one in her sleep; it was just like the tests they had practised at primary school before doing the intelligence tests you took before you went on to secondary school.

Then she had to put together a whole lot of triangles and rectangles to make a big square. That was not such fun. Sue looked at the doctor and asked, 'Are you a real doctor?'

The doctor nodded, and said he was.

'A real doctor swears an oath of secrecy, doesn't he?' asked Sue. 'I mean, he can't give away things people tell him in his consulting room?'

The doctor nodded again, and said he was silent as the grave.

'Word of honour?' asked Sue.

The doctor gave her his word of honour.

'Well then, I'm not mad!' said Sue.

The doctor said he never said she was.

'I'm not mentally disturbed either,' said Sue.

The doctor said that was what they were trying to find out.

'You don't need to try to find out. I know,' said Sue. 'I just didn't understand about advertising, but that doesn't mean I'm mad.'

The doctor assured her it didn't mean anything of the kind.

'You see, I have to live with my grandmother and my great-aunt,' Sue went on. 'Did you ever have a great-aunt?'

'I've still got one,' sighed the doctor. Sue liked him very much indeed by now.

'Well, I want to get away from them, so I thought the best thing would be for my mother to marry Dr Salamander.'

The doctor nodded. He didn't seem surprised, which was nice of him.

'And I kept on writing Mother-Mother-Mother because I didn't understand subliminal advertising properly. I thought it would get into Dr Salamander's subconscious and make him want to marry Mother.'

The doctor said he thought Sue was perfectly normal, but it would be better not to interfere in grown-ups' lives; they tended to dislike it.

'But grown-ups go interfering in my life all the time!' protested Sue. 'You don't think I *wanted* to go and live with my grandmother and my great-aunt, do you?'

No, said the doctor, he did not, but perhaps Sue might try and get on better with her great-aunt. He suggested that Grandmother might not be so important, because she was out of the house all day. 'Or if you can't get on with your great-aunt, leave her alone,' he added. 'Keep out of her way.'

'Huh!' said Sue. 'She doesn't leave *me* alone! Go indoors! Take you feet off that chair! Finish up your dinner! You can't even sit comfortably anywhere, she's always dusting and putting things straight.'

'Does she keep quoting proverbs?' asked the doctor.

Sue stared. 'How did you know?'

'I've got a great-aunt too,' the doctor reminded her.

Then he called Mother out of the waiting room and said her daughter was quite all right, no mental disturbance whatever. Mother was very pleased. And the doctor said he was sure Sue would stop writing Mother-Mother-Mother all over her school work. He added, however, 'I'm qualified to treat mental disorders, Mrs Kaufmann, but when a child's difficulties arise from her environment, and that environment cannot be changed, I'm afraid I am powerless to help.'

Mother looked puzzled. She asked, quite timidly, 'What do you mean, doctor?'

'He means Great-aunt Alice, of course!' said Sue.

Mother looked more puzzled than ever. The doctor smiled, and nodded at Sue.

Then Mother paid him for the consultation. Four

hundred Austrian schillings.

'See you some time,' said Sue to the doctor, cheerfully.

'Let's hope not!' sighed Mother. Sue shook hands with the doctor, thinking: four hundred schillings is a lot to pay, just for knowing he has a great-aunt who quotes proverbs too!

7

Day followed day, all just the same. Father had gone away on business, so there weren't even visits to him to break the monotony. Uncle Jonny had offered to take Sue out to lunch instead, and Sue tried it once, but it wasn't much fun. Uncle Jonny brought a lady with him, and Sue didn't like her. The lady's eyes were even bluer than Aunt Irma's, and her hair even blonder, and as for her smile, if she turned that on in Grandmother's shop she could have sold the entire stock in a single day. But then, Sue was not a gentleman customer buying a plant holder that looked like a brass flatiron.

Sue supposed it was Uncle Jonny's business, but if he had made a date to take her, Sue, out to lunch, then he ought to be amusing and make jokes, instead of staring all the time at a person with blue eyes and dimples who ordered grated carrot salad with lemon dressing, and kept going on about how good carrots were for the complexion.

Afterwards, Sue told J crossly, 'You should have seen him! He looked at that silly cow like the Meiers' dog looking at a bone!'

J had been out to lunch with Uncle Jonny and the carrot-eating lady once too, and she agreed with Sue about the carrot-eater: Uncle Jonny was too good for her.

Christmas was coming. You could tell from looking at the garden, where everything was bare and brown, and the ground was cold and wet. There had been a fall of snow already, but it didn't settle.

However, the most obvious sign that Christmas was coming was Great-aunt Alice. She cleaned her already clean house twice as hard as usual, and she was making cakes and biscuits for Christmas. They smelt good—for once, there was a nice smell in that house. But you could still smell the polish, in between baking times.

And Aunt Alice would not let anyone eat the cakes and biscuits, though she was baking enough to feed an orphanage. 'I can tell you, Sue,' said Aunt Irma, crossly, 'we shall have tins of the stuff hanging around till Easter, by which time they'll be hard as rocks, and then Aunt Alice will pack them up and give them to some charity or other, to be Easter presents for poor children.'

'Was Aunt Alice always so peculiar?' Sue asked.

Aunt Irma lit a cigarette. 'You know, Sue,' she said, 'that question sometimes keeps me awake at nights.' And she opened a cupboard and took out a big photograph album. 'Look,' she said. Sue looked at a picture showing a young woman who might have been Aunt Irma, but for her old-fashioned dress and the way her hair was done.

'Is it you, at a fancy dress party?' asked Sue.

'No, that's Aunt Alice when she was young,' said Aunt Irma. Sue took the album and looked, fascinated, at the page with Aunt Alice's picture. 'Where's her double chin?' she asked.

'She got her double chin later. And her blue eyes turned greyer every year, and her bosom slipped, and she grew thicker round the waist, but it all happened so gradually even Aunt Alice herself hardly noticed.' Aunt Irma put her cigarette out, and added, 'And in twenty years' time I'll look the same, and your children will be asking where your ugly old aunt got her double chin!'

There was a small disagreement about the Christmas tree in the Buchinger house almost every evening. Grandmother had what Sue called an umbrella tree. Its needles were made of green plastic and its branches of wire. It opened like an umbrella. It was about fifty centimetres tall, with an electric fairy light at the tip of each branch. Grandmother thought it was a very sensible kind of Christmas tree. Aunt Alice approved of it too, because it didn't drop its needles and there was no risk of fire. Sue and J did not like the tree. They wanted a real Christmas tree, a big one, with coloured glass balls and real candles and chocolate decorations. Aunt Irma didn't mind one way or the other; she said Christmas got on her nerves anyway. And Mother was in favour of a compromise: a real tree, but a small one, with fairy lights.

Sue had just had her report. If asked about it, she said, 'Oh, it was all right. I got several As and one B and no Cs at all.'

She was not lying. She did have several As: for gymnastics, singing, art and religious education. She had B for conduct, and she didn't have any Cs, because the rest were Ds, except E for French.

Sue did not worry too much about her report; she knew all her efforts had been spent on Dr Salamander, leaving her no time for work. She would start working harder, and her reports would improve, and luckily no one told her off about this one, because everyone knew of her recent mental disturbance. In fact, all the teachers were very kind to her, and Dr Salamander was delighted with her homework. He appeared quite beside himself with pleasure at the simplest sentences: Sue had not once written 'Mother' in her exercise book since that four-hundred-schilling visit to the doctor, not even when she really ought to have done so.

That morning Mother came into the Chamber of Horrors while J and Sue were still in bed. She said she had come to a decision, only she wasn't quite sure how to tell Grandmother and Aunt Alice yet. 'Girls, this is the first Christmas we'll be spending alone,' Mother said. 'Well, I don't exactly mean alone, but it's different from the years before. And I know there are things you don't like about this house—well, the artificial Christmas tree, and Aunt Alice and so on—so I thought. . . .'

'What did you think?' Sue sat up in bed. For a moment the mad idea crossed her mind that perhaps they were going to spend Christmas back in their old apartment with Father.

No, that was not Mother's idea, but her idea was not a bad one all the same. 'We're going away,' she said. 'Somewhere where there's snow. I'll take some of my holiday; my own nerves are all on edge, and Sue needs a rest after that neurosis of hers.'

'And I need a new pair of ski pants and an anorak,' said J. Mother agreed. Sue asked if they would be taking the Christmas presents with them, and going away before Christmas Eve.

'Yes, on the first day of school holidays,' said Mother.

That evening J and Sue went to the Soho Lady. They had arranged to meet Mother there; she said she would leave work an hour early, and they would go to the travel agency and find out about holiday accommodation.

Mother had promised to leave the shop at five-thirty, but she did not come out. Sue shifted from foot to foot; it was very cold, there was a strong wind, and Sue had forgotten her gloves. Her new coat had fur round the hem, but no pockets. She also needed the lavatory. 'You always need the lavatory when we have to wait somewhere!' J snapped.

'It's because of knowing there isn't a lavatory if I wanted one,' explained Sue. 'It makes me feel I need one.'

Sue and J went into the Soho Lady. The shop had its

Christmas decorations up. There was a huge Christmas tree, with scarves and caps and belts hanging from it, and there were silver stars dangling from the ceiling, and a loudspeaker was playing, 'Jingle bells, jingle bells, jingle all the way....' The walls were lined with mirrors, which made it difficult for Sue and J to find their way around. The mirrors were slightly concave, to make the customers look slimmer.

'Honestly, this place!' said Sue, crossly, pushing aside a silver star dangling in front of her nose. Then she fell over a pink wheelbarrow full of sweaters. She hadn't seen it, because the lighting in the Soho Lady was pink too. Sue yelped, stood the wheelbarrow back up and flung the sweaters back into it. 'Why can't they have proper rails for the clothes to hang on?' she said to J, who was standing in front of a heap of trousers.

'They're making out it's an English street market or something,' said J. Sue's yelp had attracted a sales assistant; she emerged from somewhere through a lot of wet-look coats and denim jackets, with a seductive smile. When she recognized Sue and J she turned off the seductive smile and gave them an ordinary, friendly smile. 'Your Mum's sorry, but she can't come,' she told them. 'She has to phone the T-shirt importer in Graz, and the line's always engaged.'

'But we're going to the travel agency,' said Sue.

There was a whole pile of T-shirts on a table. 'Why does Mother have to telephone, anyway?' Sue asked. 'There are plenty of T-shirts here!'

'All last season's,' the sales assistant said. 'They're out of date.'

Sue pulled a green one with a red star on the front out of the pile and asked if this one was out of date too. 'That was last spring's style,' the sales assistant told her. 'All the T-shirts had stars then. It was Che Guevara shirts in the summer, Charlie Brown shirts in the autumn, and now they all want Army T-shirts for the winter.'

Fascinated, Sue thought of her own single red-and-white striped T-shirt.

The sales assistant was just about to close the shop when a customer came in. 'Wouldn't you have thought she could have come earlier, the old bag!' said the sales assistant under her breath, smiling seductively. The customer said she wanted some small thing for her niece, maybe a pretty T-shirt, but she didn't know what the fashion was at the moment. The sales assistant smiled more seductively than ever, took the T-shirt with the star from Sue's hands and said it was the latest thing. The customer wondered whether it would fit her niece. The sales assistant was quite sure it would, though the woman had not said whether her niece was small and thin or tall and fat. The woman paid for it and took it away in a plastic carrier bag saying TOP POP SHOP.

The sales assistant said if there was one more customer she was going to scream. There weren't any more customers. She closed the shop and took Sue and J into the Soho Lady office. The office was not a top-pop sort of place at all. The walls were dirty grey, and there was only a light bulb without a shade hanging from the ceiling, no silver stars. Mother was sitting at an old desk, talking to someone on the phone and telling him about a delivery of skirts all the same size, which was apparently a bad thing, but at last she said, 'Goodbye.'

It was too late for the travel agency now, and Mother got her coat. She looked tired. 'Shall we be going to the travel agency tomorrow?' Sue asked.

'Yes, I'm sure we will,' said Mother. She didn't really sound sure.

They didn't get to the travel agency next day either.

Mother phoned to say she had to do two hours' overtime, but she tried to cheer Sue up. 'I get much more money for overtime, darling. We'll be able to have steak every day over Christmas!'

And they didn't get to the travel agency the day after either, because Mother had toothache and had to go to the dentist. You can't put off toothache till another day; Sue realized that. She sat in the Chamber of Horrors and looked gloomily at the grubby pink thing in her hands. It was the kettle holder she had crocheted at school for Mother. It was ugly; kettle holders always are. Sue had made two crochet kettle holders a year at school for the last four years. One for Christmas, one for Mother's Day. Mother never used them to hold kettles; she used them for cleaning shoes. Anyway, she didn't do the cooking in this house. Sue threw the kettle holder under the bed.

So what was she going to give Mother for Christmas? And Father, and J, and Uncle Jonny and Aunt Irma?

Sue went searching for money. She searched her red purse, her blue purse, her little leather bag and her pencil case, and came up with nineteen schillings seventy in all. But she knew she had a fifty-schilling note somewhere; she's been using it as a bookmark. She could see it, between pages 104 and 105 of the book. The question was, which book? Sue went through all her books: no fifty-schilling note anywhere. Then she remembered: she'd spent it on a brass heart on a leather thong, and the brass heart was broken now.

So she only had about enough money for wrapping paper and gold ribbon. She would just have to do the same as every year. She'd ask Father for money to buy presents for Mother and J. She'd ask Mother for money to buy presents for Father and J. Then she'd have money for a present for J twice over, so she could buy Uncle Jonny and Aunt Irma something.

Pleased to have solved her financial problems, Sue went along the corridor and looked into the kitchen. No great-aunts about. Sue opened the large kitchen dresser. The bottom shelf was crammed with cake tins and biscuit tins, ready for Christmas. Sue took a large tin out of the dresser, opened the kitchen window and climbed out into the garden, over the fence and ran to the Meiers' house. The Meiers hadn't had any home-made Christmas cakes and biscuits since Mrs Meier went away. Sue had no idea what had happened to Mrs Meier. Mother said she had died. Aunt Alice said that dreadful man Meier had driven her into a mental home. Grandmother said she had run off with another man. At all events, she hadn't been around for five years. Sue had asked Benny about his mother, but he said it was none of her business.

Sue ran through the Meiers' garden, right across the empty tulip bed, and over to Benny's window. She tapped on the glass. This was her latest craze: whenever possible she did not go through front doors, she entered houses through the window instead.

Benny was making his father a Christmas present: a standard lamp made out of the barrel of an old shot-gun, a piece of plaster for the base, and an old basket for the shade. Sue admired it.

'You know, Benny, that would cost a fortune in Grandmother's shop!'

Benny generously said that later, when they were all one family, he'd make Grandmother a horror like that once a week. 'And then we'll get rich,' he added.

'Are you sure your father isn't at all rich already?' asked Sue.

'Well, if he is he's managed to conceal it from me,' said Benny.

'You see, it would be a good idea for Mother to have a rich husband,' Sue explained. 'Then she wouldn't have to work in the Soho Lady.'

Benny was knocking nails into the basket lampshade. He spat three nails out before saying, 'No, that's no good. She'll have to go on working. I'd go up the wall if she was around all day.'

'How dare you talk about my mother like that?' said Sue indignantly. 'Don't you like my mother?'

'I don't like women at all, full stop.'

'Then why did you suggest Mother marrying your father?'

'So you can come and live with us!'

'But I'm a woman too, in case you hadn't noticed!' said Sue firmly.

Benny tapped his forehead and said, 'Nutty as a fruit cake! You're a child.'

'I'm a *girl* child,' said Sue.

'Have you got a bosom?' shouted Benny. 'Have you got painted toenails? Have you got a bottom that wobbles when you walk? Are you always wanting a man to give you money? Do you keep buying clothes? Are you always crying because someone's insulted you?'

Sue had to admit that she had and did none of these things.

'Exactly,' said Benny. 'So you're not a woman.'

Sue knew very well that Benny had the wrong end of the stick, and they had a long argument about women. It ended in compromise: Benny agreed that some women could be different, and Sue admitted that some could be the way Benny said.

'How's Operation Marriage going?' Benny asked. Operation Marriage was, of course, leading up to the wedding of that dreadful man Meier and Caroline Kaufmann. Benny had it all planned. 'We don't want to go plunging in like great flat-footed elephants,' he said. 'We want to bide our time and pick the right moment.' The moment Benny had picked was the Kaufmanns' winter holiday. 'They'll fall in love under the lights of the Christmas tree,' he had promised Sue.

There was a notebook in Benny's desk, with the whole plan worked out in it. Not on top of the desk, because Operation Marriage was a secret. Sue got the notebook out and studied the plan again. It said:

Meier & Meier . . . . Sue, J and C. Kaufmann
1. Time of meeting: Christmas holidays.
2. Meeting place: same hotel (The Green Chamois, Stoder).
3. M & M to stay at Green Chamois 23rd Dec. to 3rd Jan.
Sue to arrange same dates.
4. Sue to persuade C. Kaufmann to stay at the Chamois.
Sue to praise village of Stoder.
Sue to praise Green Chamois hotel.
Sue to give her mother brochures.
5. Remainder of operation to take place in Stoder.

Sue shut the notebook and frowned.

'Sue to do this, Sue to do that!' she muttered. 'What are *you* going to do?'

Benny said, 'Oh, really! Let me tell you, I worked hard on the project this morning. We had the day off school, and I did the most important part of the whole operation!'

Sue doubted that. Benny said, 'You idiot, I booked your rooms at the Chamois this morning! A single room and a twin-bedded room, both with balcony. It wasn't easy, either, because they're full up over Christmas. But since Dad and I have been to the Green Chamois twice a year for the last six years, the manageress let me have the rooms. She said she only did it because it was us!'

'But how did you fix it? She's in Stoder, not Vienna.'

'Rang up, of course.'

'You mean a long distance call?'

'Why not? It's easy on STD, anyone can do it.'

Sue liked to think her future brother was such a man of the world, but it did strike her he was going rather fast, booking their rooms already. Suppose Mother didn't want to go to the Chamois?

Benny assured her he had provided for all contingencies. He brought out a bundle of brochures from under his bed, at least fifty of them.

'Now, you give your mother these this evening. Tell her you wanted to save her chasing around, so you went to seven travel agencies and collected them.'

Sue leafed through the brochures. They all featured magnificent ski slopes, picturesque sunrises, pine forests, Tirolean chalets, ski instructors, dancing bears and so on. 'But what's the point?' asked Sue, bewildered. 'She'll go and pick one of these! Look: Hotel Schnepfenberg, sauna, heated swimming pool, bar, sun lounge, own ski lift, meals served at any time, all rooms with balcony, bath and toilet.'

'Look at this bit, you idiot!' Benny pointed to the last line of the brochure, the one in small print. It said: 7 days' full board, all inclusive, 2,500 schillings. But the figure had been crossed out, and 3,500 schillings was printed in large, fat type above it.

'Did it with my printing set,' explained Benny proudly. 'Looks good, doesn't it?'

'Did you alter the prices on *all* the brochures?' asked Sue, wondering if Mother might notice.

'I'm not completely dim, am I?' said Benny. 'Most of the hotels are so expensive you couldn't go to them anyway. I left the really expensive ones the way they were.'

Then Benny asked whether Sue understood, and she nodded and said, 'Yes, boss! I go home, when Mother comes in I give her the brochures. I say I wanted to save her trailing round the travel agencies. She looks at the brochures, the prices horrify her, and I tell her about this girl in my form at school who goes to a lovely inexpensive hotel every Christmas, very good value, in this lovely village called Stoder, right?'

Benny nodded. He said, 'That'll do for one day. You don't want to go too far and spoil it. You could say you'll ask your friend at school where it is she always stays, but don't go any further.'

Sue put the brochures together and opened Benny's window to climb out.

'And another thing, why do you keep coming through the window these days?' asked Benny, looking hard at Sue. 'We've got a perfectly good front door.'

Sue had one leg out of the window already. She said, 'Well, I haven't really worked it out. I expect I go through the window because it's quicker.'

'It isn't quicker, either. *And* I have to shut the window after you.'

Sue's other leg was out now. Benny shouted, 'And it gets your shoes dirty! The flower beds are all muddy!'

Sue leaned back in through the window. 'OK, now I know why I come in through the window. It's because other people don't like it! See you!'

8

Benny's plan worked like a dream. Sue had never expected it all to go so well. Mother was pleased Sue had saved her the work of chasing round the agencies. Sue kept feeding her little bits of information about Stoder and the Green Chamois, which consoled Mother for the scandalously high prices in the hotel brochures. Sue said that the girl in her form at school who always stayed at Stoder was Louise Pribil, and that almost precipitated a disaster, because Mother wanted to ring Mr Pribil and find out more details, but Sue saved the day. Luckily Benny's voice was beginning to break. Sue went to the phone and said she was dialling the Pribils' number, but actually she rang the Meiers next door. Benny answered. 'Hullo, Mr Pribil,' Sue said. 'My mother would like a word with you.'

Naturally Benny recognized Sue's voice. He told her down the phone she was too old for silly games like this. But Sue pressed on, calmly: 'You see, Louise has been telling me such nice things about Stoder at school, so my mother and my sister and I were thinking of going there ourselves, and my mother would like to know a bit more about it.'

Then Benny grasped what was going on. He chuckled. 'OK, put the lady on the line! Mr Pribil speaking, very grown up!'

'Oh, thank you, Mr Pribil,' Sue said, beckoning Mother over. Mother came to the phone and took the receiver. Sue's heart was in her mouth, but there was no need for her to worry. 'How kind of you, Mr Pribil,' Mother said, and, 'Oh, no, you really mustn't bother!' and, 'Well, if you're sure . . . yes, if you *would* be kind enough to book for us, I'd be most grateful, Mr Pribil!'

Then Mother put the phone down and said Mr Pribil had a very curious way of speaking, but he was a charming man, and he had promised Mother to book rooms for her, because though he knew the Chamois was officially full up for Christmas he was sure the manageress would oblige him.

Sue asked innocently, 'But how will we know if he did book rooms for us?'

Mother said Mr Pribil would tell Louise, who would tell Sue at school. Sue grinned happily, thinking of the poor Pribil family, who were all in bed with 'flu.

In two days' time Sue brought home a note (from Mr Pribil, of course), enclosing details of Stoder and the Green Chamois and its room prices, and a confirmation of the booking by telephone of two rooms, one single room and one twin-bedded room, for 23rd December to 3rd January. Of course the manageress had sent this confirmation to the Meiers.

Mother was making straight for the phone to thank Mr Pribil, but as Sue knew Benny was not at home she stopped Mother simply by telling her, quite truthfully, 'Mr Pribil has 'flu.' Then, of course, Mother didn't like to disturb him. However, she made Sue promise to thank Louise nicely at school tomorrow. Sue promised, and Mother gave Sue a little box of sweets the manager of the Soho Lady had given *her*, to give to Louise as a small token of gratitude.

Sue gave Benny the sweets. She thought he had earned them.

So everyone was happy, except for J. J did not want to

go to Stoder, because she had fallen in love with a brochure from a Kitzbühel hotel. Or to be precise, with the tanned ski instructor illustrated in the brochure. However, J came round in the end; she could see that Kitzbühel was too expensive. Sue's conscience was perfectly clear, because the price on that particular brochure had not been altered.

It was only a week till Christmas now. J was making long lists of the things she wanted to take. Mother had brought home two lovely pairs of ski pants from the Soho Lady, and two lovely caps and two lovely anoraks. Mother had sent the manageress of the Chamois a deposit for their rooms. There was only one thing Mother had not done yet: she had not told Grandmother and Aunt Alice and Aunt Irma they were going away. It was obvious that she was scared to. She knew Grandmother and Aunt Alice would disapprove. They both considered Christmas a big family occasion when the entire family should be together. Indeed, there always used to be trouble because Father refused to spend Christmas with Grandmother, and Mother always used to say, 'I'd love to come, but Fred doesn't want to.'

So Grandmother and Aunt Alice used to feel angry with Father and sorry for Mother.

It was different this year. Mother couldn't use Father as an excuse any more.

However, she could not postpone it any longer. It was supper time, and they were all sitting round the big kitchen table eating fried potatoes and pickled cucumbers. Nothing else, because Aunt Alice thought that if you ate sparingly for several days before Christmas you appreciated your Christmas dinner more. Aunt Alice was already discussing the Christmas dinner, wondering whether they ought to have a five kilo turkey or a six kilo turkey. Grandmother thought five. Aunt Alice thought six. 'We can always eat it up cold,' she said.

Grandmother nodded. 'With mayonnaise,' she said to Mother. 'You like that, don't you, Caroline?'

Mother swallowed. Mother cleared her throat. Mother said, 'J and Sue and I won't be here for Christmas. We're going away for a ski-ing holiday.'

'Doing what?' Aunt Irma was so surprised she swallowed a piece of pickled cucumber whole.

'Caroline, you don't mean it!' cried Grandmother. 'What nonsense! Tell me this minute you don't really mean it!'

Mother said she did mean it.

'But Caroline,' wailed Aunt Alice, 'who am I going to order the turkey for? Who's going to eat the Christmas cake? I never heard of such a thing! Haven't you got any family feeling at all?'

'Caroline, you are staying at home!' ordered Grandmother. 'In no circumstances are you going away! I forbid it!'

At that Mother exploded. She said she had a right to a life of her own, she was not a child any more, she was thirty-five years old. She said her nerves needed a rest, and that was what they would get at the Green Chamois in Stoder. She said she had nothing against Grandmother and Aunt Alice, but her poor fatherless children needed a treat; they hadn't even had a proper summer holiday. And she didn't want poor Sue going neurotic again, Mother sobbed. Then she said, blowing her nose, 'So I'm taking the girls to Stoder, and we're staying at the Green Chamois, and that's final! We've already booked our rooms.'

Grandmother got up and left the kitchen. Aunt Alice followed her. Aunt Irma stayed put. 'Goodness, Caroline, I do admire you!' she told Mother. 'I've been wanting to do that for ten years, but I never dared!'

Mother was pale. She said it was the very first time she'd ever defied Grandmother. 'No, it isn't,' said Aunt Irma. 'You defied her when you married Fred.'

Mother pulled the check tablecloth straight and muttered, almost inaudibly, 'But that's all over now.'

'And whose fault is that?' asked Aunt Irma. She added that if *she* had had a husband like Fred she would never have walked out on him. Aunt Irma liked Father; Sue thought that was the nicest thing about her, even nicer than her blue eyes and dimples. She always stood up for him. This very minute she was saying, 'Everybody's different, and a good thing too. You've got failings of your own, Caroline. Quite as many as Fred.'

Sue listened to that with satisfaction, and noticed with even more satisfaction that Mother did not burst into angry protests. She just sighed and said life was very difficult. Aunt Irma said life was only difficult if you made difficulties for yourself. J nodded, as if she understood what they were on about. Sue left the supper table and went to see Benny. For a change she went out of the front door. Walking down the gravel path and past the lighted sitting room window, she saw Grandmother in there, marching up and down, her face grim. Sue giggled. 'Left, two, three, four, about turn, quick march, Sergeant-Major! Lost the battle this time!'

Had Sue been able to guess the decision her grandmother was making she would not have giggled, she would have fainted right away. But Sue was not a mind reader. She ran happily to the fence. Mr Joseph came to meet her, barking with delight. That dreadful man Meier was in the garden too. Sue stopped to discuss the best time for planting tulip bulbs with him. These days Sue seized every opportunity to talk to Mr Meier. After all, she'd have to get to know him. So far, she was very pleased with her choice. But she had not decided whether to call him Father or Uncle or Mr Meier. Well, she couldn't call him Father, she had one of them already. Mr Meier was too formal. Uncle sounded silly. 'What's your first name, Mr Meier?' she asked.

'Benjamin, of course,' said Mr Meier. 'Where else do you think Benny got such a funny name?'

'I like Benjamin,' said Sue. She went into the Meiers' house and asked Benny if she could call his father Benjamin. Benny said she could.

We have already seen Grandmother marching up and down the sitting room, taking a decision. As sergeant-majors always have to think for the men under their command, she had taken it not just for herself, but for Great-aunt Alice and Aunt Irma too. However, Grandmother kept quiet about it. She stalked round the house in grim silence. J said, 'I bet she's going to disinherit us.'

'Is that a bad thing?' asked Sue.

J had no idea if it was bad or not. 'If there were going to be quarrels here the whole time, we might just as well have stayed with Father, if you ask me,' she said.

Father came back from his business trip three days before Christmas. Sue and J met him to go Christmas shopping. They were in one of Vienna's big shopping streets, it was raining a little and snowing a little, and there was a sharp wind blowing. Father had just earned quite a lot of money fairly easily, so he was generous over Christmas presents. He had even bought a present for Benny, a genuine American policeman's gun belt. Sue tried it on. Father asked, 'Have you two got anything for the Sergeant-Major?'

Sue and J had not intended to give Grandmother a present, but Christmas shopping tends to fill you with goodwill. After all, Christmas is a time of peace. Grandmother ought to have a present. But what? J had a good idea. She said Hufnagel & Hufnagel, Ladies' Fashions, was not far off, and Grandmother bought all her clothes there. Sue agreed that Mrs Hufnagel would know Grandmother's taste, and help them choose a scarf or something for her.

Hufnagel & Hufnagel was not in the least like the Soho Lady. Chandeliers hung from the high ceiling, three large ones, two medium-sized ones and three little ones, the clothes hung tidily on rails behind brown velvet curtains, and the place was quiet as a church. Sue, J and Father stood on a brown Persian carpet under the chandeliers. Father coughed to try and attract someone's attention. He did. A lady came down the dark brown wooden staircase from the upper floor of the shop. She was enormous, as tall as Father and twice as broad, and she was swathed in white jersey with beads on it. Her faded yellow hair was plaited, and the plait wound three times round her head. This lady was Mrs Hufnagel senior, no less. Two of her assistants came downstairs after her. They were small and thin and mousy. There was a hunted look on Father's face.

However, he explained that he was Mrs Buchinger's son-in-law, and he was looking for a scarf for her. When Father said 'son-in-law' Mrs Hufnagel's eyebrows rose at least two centimetres. She seemed to know all about recent events in the Buchinger family. The mousy ladies kept well away from Father, looking at him suspiciously.

Mrs Hufnagel senior brought out a silk scarf. Just one. It was pale grey with dark grey roses on it and mauve rose leaves. There was a deep black border round it. The effect was dismal, though Father seemed to like it. 'A granite rose bed,' he said appreciatively.

Mrs Hufnagel senior took this for a compliment. She

unbent slightly. She even made a request: did Mrs Buchinger's son-in-law have his car here? Yes, he did have his car here. Would Mrs Buchinger's son-in-law be kind enough to take the Buchinger ladies' things with him, so that they did not have to drive into town specially to fetch them?

'What things?' asked J.

'The ladies' ski outfits,' said Mrs Hufnagel senior.

'There must be some mistake!' cried Sue.

Mrs Hufnagel senior shook her head and signed to the mousy ladies, who scuttled away. They came back with two pairs of ski pants, two anoraks, several pullovers and caps and scarves. Half the things were sky-blue and the other half were pink. Mrs Hufnagel called one lot '*bleu*' and the other lot '*rosé*', and explained that the *bleu* things were for Grandmother and the *rosé* things for dear Miss Alice. One of the mousy ladies added a mound of *eau-de-nil* silk to the pile.

'For *après ski*,' announced Mrs Hufnagel senior. She displayed two pairs of silk pyjamas embroidered with Christmas roses. Holding the top half of one up to her huge chest, she whispered, '*Voilà*! The *dernier cri*! Though I am not sure,' she added, 'whether a little village like Stoder has a hotel suitable for the wearing of *haute couture* models like these.'

Sue saw it all. She did not fly into a temper; no temper she could have flown into would have expressed the way she was feeling.

Father said, stammering, that he didn't have room for the things in his car. Mrs Hufnagel registered this with some indignation. J ran out of the shop, with Sue after her. Father paid for the granite rose bed and followed them. They all made for the car. As he started up, Father said, 'Oh lord—is there anything I can do to help?' He sounded at a loss.

'Buy me a gun!' muttered J.

'I'm afraid shooting grandmothers and great-aunts is against the law,' said Father.

'Very funny!' snapped J.

Father drove to Grandmother's house. Sue and J ought to have said goodbye to him particularly nicely, since they wouldn't be seeing him again before Christmas. Obviously nothing nice occurred to J. She said sarcastically, 'Happy Christmas, Father dear. Oh, think how happy you've made your daughters. Oh, isn't everything just lovely! Thanks *so* much!'

She seized all the parcels, got out of the car and slammed the door. Sue stayed put. She whispered, 'Father, J doesn't really mean it!'

'She has a point,' said Father.

'What will *you* be doing over Christmas?' asked Sue.

'Nothing much,' said Father.

'Bloody hell,' muttered Sue; she didn't usually swear, but she knew saying 'bloody hell' was a good way to stop herself crying.

'It's late,' said Father.

Sue nodded. She got out. Father wound down the window and called after her, 'Have a good time.'

Then he drove off.

Sue thought: what a silly thing to say! Have a good time! Good! There wasn't going to be anything good about it!

Sue went towards the house. The gravel on the path was wet, and Sue dug the toes of her shoes into it as she walked, kicking up the little pebbles and muttering bitterly, 'Have a good time a good time good time good time....'

Mother's coat was hanging in the hall, so she was home. There was not so much for her to do at the Soho Lady in the last few days before Christmas; the feverish Christmas shopping rush was over, and most people were at home cooking for the Christmas festivities.

Sue heard her sister's voice, and followed it to Mother's room. Sue knocked; you always knocked in the Buchinger household, though you didn't wait to be told to come in. You knocked and opened the door directly. Sue opened the door. J was standing in front of Mother, waving her arms about and shouting. J was saying a lot— everything, in fact, How awful, horrible, beastly life was these days! And to put the lid on it, Grandmother and Aunt Alice were coming to Stoder too!

At first Mother thought J must have made a mistake. It was ridiculous! But after hearing a detailed description of the ski outfits in *bleu* and *rosé* Mother was ready to believe the story. However, she explained, she could hardly forbid anyone, even her own mother, to go to Stoder. Just then Aunt Irma came home. 'Come here, would you, Irma?' Mother called.

Aunt Irma came in. 'Are Mother and Aunt Alice going to Stoder?' Mother asked.

Aunt Irma nodded unhappily. 'I've got to go too,' she said. 'First of all Mother was furious you three were going away, because it showed such a lack of family feeling. Then she said it was because you were all under such nervous strain, unable to think clearly. She said it was her duty to look after you, so she decided to go too. It's supposed to be a special Christmas surprise for you.'

Mother's shoulders drooped wearily. 'Children, there's nothing we can do about it!'

'Why not?' cried Sue. 'Tell her we want to be alone! Tell her it's not because of the mountain air we're going away! Tell her we can think perfectly clearly, and she's got to leave us in peace!'

Mother said she couldn't possible say that.

'You're a coward!" shouted J.

'All right then, I'm a coward!' cried Mother. 'I can't help it. I've tried, but I can't. And I'm fond of my mother! After all, she can't help being the way she is. And I can't help being the way I am!'

'And I can't help being the way I am either!' shouted Sue, leaving Mother's room. She slammed the door so hard behind her that the pictures on the walls shook.

Sue was going to visit Benny. Just as she was climbing the fence, Grandmother opened the garden gate. She was carrying a parcel. Aunt Alice was panting along behind her with another parcel. Ski boots, I bet, thought Sue. She was quite right. Hidden behind the currant bushes, Sue heard Grandmother and Aunt Alice talking.

Grandmother said, 'You're too timid, that's your trouble!'

Aunt Alice wailed, 'You can't teach an old dog new tricks!'

Grandmother said, 'You'll enjoy it when we get there.'

Aunt Alice said, 'Don't count your chickens before they're hatched.'

Grandmother said, 'I shall sit at the front of the toboggan, and you will sit at the back, and all you'll have to do is brake.'

Great-aunt Alice's reply could not be heard, for the wind blew it away, but it must have been another proverb, because Grandmother shouted crossly, 'And I hope to goodness a snowstorm blows some of those proverbs out of your head!'

Sue went to Benny's window and knocked. Benny opened it. Sue climbed in and Benny asked for news. Sue said there wasn't any. She dared not tell Benny about Grandmother and Aunt Alice; he would say she had to stop them coming, and he wouldn't realize there was nothing she could do about it. He'd probably abandon

Operation Marriage entirely.

So Sue said nothing; she guided the conversation away from Operation Marriage by asking Benny what happens to a minus sign in a round bracket if there is another minus sign outside the bracket, and what difference it makes if there's a square bracket and another minus sign in front of the whole lot? Sue had judged it well; Benny plunged enthusiastically into explaining brackets and minus signs, and Sue pretended to be listening.

Next day was the last day of term. In Fiery Salamander's lesson they sang carols, and Karl Novotny, who read aloud well, read a piece about Christmas not just being presents, but peace and goodwill in our hearts, and how giving was better than receiving, and the world was full of inhumanity and strife, and we should all think of that at Christmas time. Sue wondered whether the inhumanity and strife would all stop if she didn't get any Christmas presents. She couldn't really see the connection. Then they went home.

That evening Sue had to pack her case. Later Grandmother told them her very special Christmas surprise. Mother actually pretended to be pleased.

Grandmother added, 'And by a stroke of great good luck, we managed to book a room in the Green Chamois ourselves!'

Grandmother told them, 'The manageress offered us a little room which she doesn't usually let. However, Irma must go to another hotel.'

That really put the lid on it! Sue had thought the Green Chamois was absolutely full, so that at least she'd be a road and several buildings away from Grandmother.

As might have been expected, immediately after revealing her surprise Grandmother took over the planning of the entire holiday. She said it was ridiculous for Mother to propose taking her old Volkswagen.

'My car and Irma's will be quite enough,' she said.

'The presents can go in Irma's boot,' she said.

'One case each will do,' she said.

'And we'll take my Christmas tree,' she said.

'And open the Christmas presents in my room,' she said.

'Caroline can travel in Irma's car and the girls in mine,' she said.

'We'll take the motorway to Salzburg and then go through Weiler,' she said.

'We'll start at eleven-thirty,' she said.

'Irma will drive behind me,' she said.

And Mother and Aunt Irma kept nodding.

Sue went to bed. Just before going to sleep she realized she'd only packed one pair of knickers and no gloves. While she was wondering whether to go and pack some more knickers and a pair of gloves, she dropped off.

9

On the morning of December 23rd the sun was shining and the sky was blue. It was fourteen degrees above freezing, and there was a warm wind blowing. Sue thought grimly that they might have known it: with this spring-like weather there wouldn't even be any good snow for ski-ing!

Benny and that dreadful man Meier had left for Stoder first thing in the morning, because the roads are emptier then. Benny had left a letter for Sue in the box by the garden gate. It said, 'Dear Sue, See you soon. Things can't go wrong now! I'm looking forward to this! Benny.'

At eleven-thirty the family was ready to start. Aunt Alice, in her pink ski outfit, went round the house checking that all the windows were closed and the gas turned off and the central heating turned right down and there were no taps dripping. Then she locked all three locks on the front door. Grandmother, in her sky-blue ski outfit, turned the key in the garden gate three times.

Sue tried to nip into Aunt Irma's car, but Mother whispered, in tones of desperation, 'Please, Sue, *please*!'

So Sue got into Grandmother's car. Grandmother issued final instructions.

'Don't talk much, and don't talk too loud. Don't drop any biscuit crumbs. You can look out of the window at the countryside! And keep your heads still, or I can't see out of the rear view mirror.'

Sue and J nodded.

You could say what you liked about Grandmother, but no one could have claimed she was a bad driver. She drove well and she drove fast. Too fast for Aunt Alice, who begged, 'Hasten slowly!'

Grandmother snapped that if she had decided to drive at 140 k.p.h. no one was going to persuade her to do otherwise. Neither Aunt Alice nor that person in the BMW who was trying to overtake, even though she had already signalled that she was pulling out herself.

Just after Linz they lost sight of Aunt Irma's car. Aunt Irma couldn't keep up with Grandmother. Grandmother did not wait for her, she drove on to Salzburg. Then they went straight on to Weiler, where Sue said, 'I need the lavatory.'

Grandmother drove into the main square of Weiler, but you were not allowed to park there. 'It's only another half an hour's drive to Stoder,' Grandmother said. 'You can last that long.'

Sue said she couldn't, not possibly. She'd been needing the lavatory ever since Linz. Then she began to groan and shift about on the seat. Grandmother stopped in the middle of the no-parking zone. There was a policeman on the pavement who told Grandmother she couldn't park there. Grandmother told the policeman about her granddaughter's urgent needs. He was sympathetic, but he said they must hurry.

Aunt Alice, Sue and J trotted off behind Grandmother into the Posthouse. J wailed, 'I'm thirsty.'

Grandmother announced that they might as well have a cup of tea. 'But the car's in a no-parking zone!' said Aunt Alice.

Grandmother dismissed that. She said no policeman could know how long her granddaughter needed to spend in the lavatory. Sue followed the arrows to the Ladies while the others went into the main room of the Posthouse. When Sue came back Grandmother was arguing with the man behind the counter, who was saying he could only do tea in teabags.

Grandmother refused to drink tea made from teabags. The man said he was sorry, that was all they had. J said she'd rather have a coke anyway, but Grandmother was adamant. She was not stopping in a place where they made tea from teabags, and if J was thirsty she must just put up with it.

'Poor kids,' muttered the man. Grandmother inquired if he would care to repeat that, and then stalked out. Sue, J and Aunt Alice had to follow her.

Half an hour later they drew up outside the Green Chamois. Grandmother liked the look of the outside. 'Nice, solid, unpretentious place,' she said approvingly.

Aunt Alice pointed out that appearances could be deceptive, but they were not. The Green Chamois was nice inside too, with pinewood, wrought iron, and blue and white check curtains. The manageress was rather like a country version of Mrs Hufnagel senior. She and Grandmother took to each other at once. She took three room keys off the board and led Grandmother up to the first floor. Sue and J followed them. Aunt Alice stayed downstairs, inspecting the Green Chamois for dust and dirt.

Number 12 was Mother's single room. Number 13 was Sue and J's twin-bedded room. Number 23 was the room Grandmother had booked, later, for herself and Aunt Alice. Numbers 12 and 13 were lovely. Number 23 was horrible. It contained an ancient bed, a sofa, a lop-sided cupboard and a stool; there was no room for any more furniture. The manageress apologized.

'Of course I never let it in the normal way. No running water, you see, and no heating. But you were so insistent, ma'am!'

Sue grinned maliciously. She could well believe it: it served Grandmother right! But Grandmother was examining Number 23, unmoved, and saying, 'Oh, it's not so bad. The children will be quite all right in here!' And then she went back along the long corridor and took possession of the nice room. Number 13.

J flung herself down on the sofa and hammered at it with her fists. 'This is too much!' she sobbed. 'I won't put up with it, I won't!'

'What are you going to do about it, then?'

'Tell Mother!'

'Mother?'

'Yes, Mother!'

'And what will *she* do about it?' inquired Sue.

'Nothing!' sobbed J.

'So there you are,' said Sue.

Sue tried to unpack her case. She wriggled her way in between the sofa and the bed over to the cupboard. The cupboard door wouldn't open more than a crack because the sofa was in the way. Sue tried pushing the sofa further away from it, but then you couldn't open the door of the room.

'Oh, never mind!' said J. Sue gave up the attempt. She climbed over the sofa, digging her knee into J's stomach by mistake. J yelled, and Sue apologized. 'I'm going to look for Benny,' she said.

'Who?'

'Benjamin Meier junior.'

'Where on earth d'you expect to find him?' asked J curiously, sitting up.

'Room Number 10.'

'Why?'

'He's staying there. With his father.'

'Did you know in advance?' asked J.

'I planned the whole thing!' Sue announced.

102

'Oh, heaven help us!' groaned J. Then she added, 'Planned *what* whole thing?'

Sue should really have kept her mouth shut, but she didn't. She said, 'I planned for Mother and Mr Meier to fall in love and get married, and then we'll move into the Meiers' house. It's a very good idea.'

Sue waited for praise, or at least a word of appreciation. But J was offering neither. Far from it. She yelled, 'You're absolutely nuts!' Then she added, apologetically, 'Well, it's not surprising.'

'I am not nuts!' said Sue. 'Why are you being so horrible? Don't you want to go and live with Mr Meier?'

'The question just doesn't arise,' sighed J. 'Do you honestly think he and Mother are going to fall in love, when they haven't been able to stand the sight of each other for thirty years?'

'We'll soon find out,' said Sue, leaving the room in search of the door of Number 10. She heard J's mocking laughter behind her.

The door of Number 10 was right by the pinewood staircase. Sue wondered whether to knock. While she was wondering two things happened at the same time. First: Benny Meier and his father started up the stairs from the ground floor. Second: the door of Number 13 opened and Grandmother came out into the corridor, bound for the lavatory.

Sue fled up the stairs to the second floor and stood there, holding her breath, and watching the corridor below through the heart-shaped holes in the banisters.

She saw Grandmother, in search of the lavatory, pass the head of the stairs up to the first floor. Grandmother glanced down, saw Benny and that dreadful man Meier, and froze. That dreadful man Meier and Benny stared back. Then Benny let out a yell.

'No!' cried Benny. 'No!'

'Oh, for the lord's sake!' said Mr Meier. 'This is too much!'

'Really!' said Grandmother. 'What impertinence!' And she went on her way towards the lavatory. Benny and Mr Meier came up the rest of the stairs and went into their room. Sue stayed behind her heart-shaped peephole, waiting till the cistern flushed, the hinges of the lavatory door squealed, and Grandmother marched out. The door of Number 13 closed behind her. Sue slipped down the stairs, crept up to the door of Number 13, put her ear to the keyhole and listened.

'Dear me, dear me, whatever is wrong, Henrietta?' Aunt Alice was saying plaintively. 'You're so pale! Something must have scared you, you're trembling!'

And Sue heard Grandmother say, 'I have just seen that dreadful man Meier and his son!'

Aunt Alice: 'You're imagining things! A hallucination! It comes of the change of air, you know. Sensitive people are subject to hallucinations.'

Grandmother: 'Hallucination my foot! I saw the two Meiers!'

Aunt Alice: 'In the flesh?'

Grandmother: 'Definitely in the flesh!'

Aunt Alice: 'What a strange coincidence!'

Grandmother: 'Coincidence! Humph! Someone is responsible for this!'

Sue jumped nervously. This could get rather unpleasant. But then she sighed in relief. Grandmother was saying, 'I shall demand an explanation from Irma. Or Caroline, I'm not sure which.'

Sue crept off to the door of Number 10. It was comic, really! Grandmother seemed to think Mother or Aunt Irma had arranged to meet Mr Meier here on purpose!

She did not have to put her ear to the keyhole of Number 10. The voices of Benny and his father carried easily through the door, with Mr Joseph contributing the occasional bark.

Benny: 'Honestly, Dad, I promise I had no idea! I thought I'd have a heart attack myself when I saw the old bag: I can't make it out.'

Mr Meier: 'Well, it's more than I can take! I just walk up a staircase, doing nobody any harm, and there I am face to face with my *bête noire*!'

Benny: 'Do you think Sue's Great-aunt Alice is here too?'

Mr Meier: 'You bet your life she is! They never go about alone, they hunt in packs. The whole lot will be here: the old bag, the good lady with the proverbs, our pretty dimpled Irma, fat old Caroline and those two giggling girls!'

(Sue ground her teeth when he said 'fat old Caroline', and ground them again when he said 'giggling girls'.)

Benny: 'Sue doesn't giggle. J's not so bad, either.'

(Sue nodded, feeling better.)

Mr Meier: 'Well, if they're not so bad now, they soon will be! No one could stay normal in that family. That grandmother of theirs is a steamroller. Flattens everything in her path. When I was a boy I used to tremble at the mere sight of her.'

Benny: 'I don't.'

Mr Meier: 'Well, she's getting on now. Had to turn the pressure down a bit.'

Benny: 'And Sue's mother is very nice.'

Mr Meier: 'Ho, ho! Caroline, nice? I can still remember her as a child: fat and tearful and full of grievances. Never a word to say for herself. We used to call her "I'll-tell-my-mother-of-you". Once I rubbed mud all over her and put some in her mouth, and do you know what she said to me?'

Benny: 'Oh, Dad, how should I know what a fat little

girl said to you thirty years ago?'

Mr Meier: 'Well, guess! Go on, guess!'

Benny: 'I expect she said she'd tell her mother of you.'

Mr Meier: 'No, she said, "You're a naughty, naughty boy!"'

Benny: 'So she did have a word to say for herself!'

Mr Meier: 'Look, let's not discuss that family of vampires any longer, right? It makes me feel quite ill!'

Sue had heard more than enough. Gloomily, she made her way back to Number 23. J was still lying on the sofa. There was a 15 watt bulb without any shade hanging from the ceiling. Sue said, 'Let's go out and wait for Mother, J.'

J got up and took their new Soho Lady anoraks out of her case. The anoraks were orange, with a big yellow star on the back. J muttered, slipping hers on, 'I was so looking forward to this, and now it's all spoilt!'

'Ought we to tell Grandmother we're going out?' asked Sue.

J shook her head. She said she was not going to tell Grandmother anything, ever again. She was never going to *look* at Grandmother ever again. So far as she was concerned, Grandmother didn't exist.

Just as Sue and J reached the big entrance gate of the Green Chamois, Aunt Irma's car drove up. Mother and Aunt Irma got out, opened the boot and took out Mother's case and the tin with the Christmas cake in it and the boxes of Christmas presents. Then Aunt Irma shut the boot. She was looking rather anxious. She asked Mother, 'Do you think I ought to go up and tell them?'

'No, I do not,' said Mother. 'If you do you'll change your mind!'

Aunt Irma took two parcels out of the car. 'Here,' she said. 'My presents for Mother and Aunt Alice. The big one is Mother's and the little one is Aunt Alice's, and I've left the invoices inside in case they want to change them.'

'Yes, yes, all right!' said Mother. 'For heaven's sake get a move on!'

'Hi, girls!' said Aunt Irma. 'See you, Caroline!' And she got into her car and drove off.

Sue and J helped Mother get the boxes and parcels up to Number 12. Sue looked inquiringly at J. Her glance of inquiry meant: What was all that about? What's Aunt Irma up to? J shrugged her shoulders, looking equally baffled.

In Room 12, Mother looked out of the window at the balcony and the dark, starry sky.

'Lovely!' she said. Then she asked, 'Well, are you comfortably settled in, girls?'

So Sue and J told her. About the bedrooms, and how they had been switched. And Grandmother. Or they did not exactly tell her: they shouted, and grumbled, and complained, and uttered wild threats. Mother sank wearily on to her bed. 'Just let me get my breath back, children!' she groaned. 'Surely it can't be that bad!'

Sue and J did not feel inclined to let Mother get her breath back. They told her it *was* that bad, and worse! They said it had never been as bad as this—and then the door opened and Grandmother came in.

'Ah, here you are at last, Caroline!' she said. She turned to Sue and J. 'You are making a noise like a cartload of monkeys!' she told them. 'What in the world is the matter?'

At this something snapped inside J. She could feel it, quite plainly. A gentle little pop, like a balloon bursting. J's balloon was full of grievances against Grandmother, and they came flooding out of the burst balloon. J had no need to stop and pick her words; she only had to open her mouth and let fly.

'I'll tell you what the matter is! The matter is you're so horrible! You simply pinched our room! You never ask anyone if they agree with you, you just do whatever you like and everyone else has to put up with it! You think the whole world revolves around you. I don't like you at all! I hate you! Give us back our room!'

Grandmother's jaw dropped. She said, 'You surely don't expect me and Aunt Alice, poor thing, to sleep in a poky boxroom?'

J shouted, 'We booked the nice room, and it's ours. You booked the poky boxroom and it's yours!'

Grandmother bellowed, 'Julia, kindly control yourself at once! What a way to speak to me!'

J glared at Grandmother. More quietly, Grandmother said, 'You ought to be glad I let you have the smaller room. It's remarkably cheap, and your mother has enough money problems as it is.' At this point Grandmother looked all round the room, as if in search of something. 'Where is Irma?' she asked.

Mother was lying flat on the bed, her eyes closed. 'Irma's gone,' she said.

'What do you mean, *gone*?' inquired Grandmother. 'She knows quite well I like to have supper at seven-thirty! So when is she coming? Where is she? Has she gone to her own hotel? She might have waited till after supper!'

Mother stayed put, her eyes still closed. She said, quietly, 'I just told you, Mother, she's gone. She won't be here for supper.'

'What on earth do you mean? Have you all gone crazy?'

Grandmother went over to the bed and shook Mother's shoulder. Mother opened her eyes and sat up. She said, 'Irma and I stopped for coffee just outside Salzburg, and we met Dr Sterkl and his sister, and Philip Beierl, and a few others. They were all off to a chalet in the Tirol.'

Grandmother interrupted. 'This is quite irrelevant. What in the world has Dr Sterkl got to do with my supper? What has a chalet in the Tirol got to do with Irma?'

Mother sighed. 'Dr Sterkl has nothing to do with your supper. Nor does the chalet. But they have plenty to do with Irma. Irma drove me here, and then she went on to join Dr Sterkl's party. In the chalet. I persuaded her to go.'

Suddenly it was perfectly quiet in Number 12. The only sound you could hear was Grandmother, breathing hard.

Sue glanced at J. J was standing there, grinning like a wicked little imp. Sue looked at Mother. Mother was white as a sheet, her eyelids were fluttering and her nose looked pinched. Sue looked at Grandmother. Grandmother was standing in the middle of the room, breathing heavily, and her throat was blotchy red. 'The impertinence of it!' she gasped. 'The whole lot of you! Christmas is a family occasion! A family occasion! Families ought to....'

Mother said, shrilly, 'Yes, a family occasion! And why shouldn't Irma have a family of her own some time? She'd like to. She and Dr Sterkl, maybe.'

'Ridiculous!' screeched Grandmother. 'Irma has a perfectly good family already.'

'Oh, no,' said Mother. 'Oh, no, she hasn't. You have a family, the rest of us don't.'

It was quite quiet in the room again, except for Grandmother's heavy breathing, which was slowly becoming calmer. She said, 'We will now go and have supper.'

Mother got off the bed, took a comb out of her handbag, went over to the mirror and did her hair. There was a knock at the door, and Aunt Alice came in. Sue stared at Aunt Alice; Sue began to giggle, to laugh, to squeal hysterically. She couldn't help it. It felt so good to see something really funny, after such a tense, unpleasant day. The funny thing in this case was Great-aunt Alice, wearing her *eau-de-nil* silk *après ski* pyjamas. Sue had been staggered by this garment when she saw it in Hufnagel & Hufnagel, but it was only on Aunt Alice you saw it in its full glory. Aunt Alice looked like a mountain of pistachio ice cream. But funniest of all were the Christmas roses, marching in single file up Aunt Alice's trouser legs and down her sleeves, in the direction of her stomach, where they all met. There was a massed band of Christmas roses on Aunt Alice's stomach.

'Take that thing off!' spat Grandmother.

'Oh, but I thought . . .' stammered Aunt Alice.

'Then don't think!' Grandmother told her. 'Go and change! Irma has gone. Gone to the Tirol with Dr Sterkl!'

Aunt Alice looked shocked. 'I don't know what young people are coming to these days!' she whispered.

Grandmother looked at her watch. 'We shall meet in the dining room in five minutes' time,' she said.

And so saying, Grandmother left Number 12, propelling the mountain of pistachio ice cream ahead of her.

Mother got the sponge bag out of her case and gave it to J. Sue made for the door. She wanted to get out; for one thing, she wasn't too keen on washing, and for another, it was high time she had a word with Benny.

'Sue,' said Mother. Her voice was still high and trembling. 'Sue, you will be downstairs in five minutes, won't you?'

Sue nodded, and closed the door behind her. Benny was standing by the pinewood stairs. He beckoned to her.

'Follow me,' he whispered. He went along the corridor to a door saying PRIVATE. Benny opened the door, and Sue slipped through it after him. They were in a little room full of sheets and towels. Sue and Benny sat down on a pile of them.

'This is the linen room,' said Benny. Sue nodded. 'No one will disturb us here,' he said. Sue nodded again.

'Crikey, what a mess!' said Benny. Sue nodded for the

110

third time.

'How did it happen?' asked Benny. 'Can you explain?'
He didn't sound too friendly. Sue nodded once more and
said, 'They came for a Christmas surprise.'

Benny sighed. 'Well, it's put a spoke in the wheels of
Operation Marriage all right. My father had a nasty
shock, and it'll take him some time to recover. There's
nothing we can do today, and anyway I'm flat out. Your
aged relatives are a bit much!'

They heard a loud voice in the corridor. 'Benny! Where
are you?'

Sue and Benny emerged from the linen room. Mr Meier
was standing there.

'Not another Buchinger!' he said sarcastically. Sue
planted herself in front of Mr Meier, stood on tiptoe and
informed him, 'Mr Meier, my name is Kaufmann, and
kindly don't forget it!'

'Sure, Miss Buchinger, your name is Kaufmann,' said
Mr Meier, and he made for the pine staircase, with Benny
after him.

Sue glanced into Numbers 12 and 13, which were both
empty, so her family had gone down to the dining room.
Sue hesitated, thinking of the state of her fingernails,
which were rather black. She tried cleaning the nails of
her left hand with the nail of her right forefinger, and that
worked quite well, but she couldn't get the nails of her
right hand clean. There was something sticky under them
that wouldn't come out.

J appeared on the stairs. 'Hey, they sent me to find you,'
she said. 'Come on.'

The dining room was very large and very empty. Most
of the guests coming to the Green Chamois for Christmas
wouldn't arrive till next day. There was a large Christmas
tree with fairy lights and tinsel beside the dining room
door. Benny and his father were sitting at one table, and

Grandmother, Aunt Alice and Mother were sitting at another. There were about twenty empty tables covered with white cloths between them. J grinned and whispered, 'How's the wedding plan coming along?'

Sue did not answer. The twenty empty tables did look rather bleak.

'What kept you?' Grandmother asked. She looked only too willing to unleash all her pent-up fury on Sue. However, Sue had a good line of defence. 'I had to spend a long time in the lavatory,' she said. 'I've got diarrhoea.'

'One does not mention such things at table,' said Grandmother.

Sue smiled sweetly. 'I didn't want to mention it. You asked.'

This silenced Grandmother, but it turned out not to have been such a good idea after all, because Mother cancelled her order for roast pork for Sue, and despite her protests she got sieved carrots, rusks and camomile tea instead. Then Grandmother looked around and picked a new victim. Mother.

'And now, Caroline, I require an explanation!' said Grandmother. 'What is that dreadful man Meier doing here?'

Mother looked around, bewildered. She had not even noticed Mr Meier yet. Grandmother pointed dramatically at the Meiers' table. Mother groaned, 'Oh no! What next!'

'Caroline, do you mean to tell me you knew nothing about this? It was *your* idea to come to Stoder for....'

Something had to be done to interrupt Grandmother, and at once. Sue asked, very loudly, 'Will Aunt Irma have got to the Tirol yet?'

Grandmother did indeed stop cross-examining Mother. 'I do not wish to hear another word about your Aunt Irma,' she told Sue, 'or I shall leave the table!' As if that

112

was a threat!

'Is Aunt Irma in love with Dr Sterkl, or Philip Beierl, or both of them?' Sue persisted. The fork in her grandmother's hand trembled.

'Look, I only want to know who Aunt Irma's in love with!'

'Leave the table at once!' cried Grandmother.

That really did infuriate Sue. She ground her teeth. 'I thought *you* were going to leave the table if I said another word about Aunt Irma,' she pointed out.

'That's right,' said J. 'That's what Grandmother said.'

Grandmother dropped her fork and took a deep breath, ready to let fly. Suddenly Aunt Alice said, 'Why beholdest thou the mote that is in thy brother's eye?'

'What?' said Grandmother, forgetting to let fly.

Aunt Alice smiled, shook her head, and went on, 'Many a true word spoken in jest! Nothing to make a song and dance about. Early to bed, early to rise, makes a man healthy, wealthy and wise. We can't see the wood for the trees, you know, and people who live in glass houses shouldn't throw stones.'

'Alice!' said Grandmother, threateningly.

'It's love that makes the world go round,' murmured Aunt Alice.

'Oh, do be quiet, Aunt Alice!' wailed Mother.

'Yes, we all have our crosses to bear,' whispered Aunt Alice, and she rose from her chair and left the dining room. She appeared to be floating just above the ground.

'Has she gone crazy?' asked J.

Grandmother got up and said she'd better see to Aunt Alice. She marched off.

Sue left the dining room too. She didn't want any sieved carrots and rusks, and she certainly did not wish to answer any questions Mother might ask about the Meiers and how they came to be in this very hotel.

At the dining room door Sue met a waiter with an enormous dish of ice cream which had a peach on top. The waiter was carrying this magnificent concoction to the Meiers' table.

Sue ran upstairs, along the corridor, to the poky little room. Her open case was lying on the sofa. Sue kicked it. The case slipped down between the sofa and the bed and snapped shut, with bits of socks, sweater sleeves and belts hanging out of it. Sue crouched on the hard sofa, reaching down. The floor was cold to her hands when they touched it. She pulled her knees up to her chin. She had to stretch her neck to get her chin on her knees; it was uncomfortable. Sue was glad it was uncomfortable. If I stretched my chin just a little further forward, thought Sue, all the muscles of my throat would crack. And my windpipe and oesophagus and neck would break too, and I'd be dead.

Sue tried sticking her chin out that fatal bit further. It hurt, and something clicked inside her neck, but nothing broke. Sue sat up and rubbed her throat with both hands. No good, she'd just have to go to sleep.

Sue took off her jeans, pullover, blouse and socks. Where were her pyjamas? In her case, and the case was down the crack between the sofa and the bed. Sue felt no desire to dig her pyjamas out. She just got into bed with nothing on. She had gooseflesh. Her pillow seemed to be full of sawdust, and her quilt was like damp cotton wool, and her blanket was made of corrugated iron. J's pillow and quilt looked much softer and warmer. Sue put out her hand and grabbed J's pillow. Yes, it *was* softer. She put out her hand for J's blanket too. It was made of corrugated iron, like her own, but two bits of corrugated iron are warmer than one. She settled down to go to sleep.

Less than an hour later she was woken by J, shaking her. 'You little horror, give me back my blanket and pillow!'

114

Sue clung to the blanket and the pillow. J snatched them away. Sue tried to retrieve them. A silent but determined fight began.

Then the door of the room opened and Aunt Alice looked in. She was wearing a bright pink dressing-gown. She whispered, 'The lesser of two evils, my dears! A stitch in time saves nine!'

Sue and J stopped fighting and gazed at Aunt Alice in alarm. Aunt Alice nodded kindly to them, and closed the door behind her. J listened to her retreating footsteps. She sighed. 'That was all we needed!'

However, the apparition of Aunt Alice had put a stop to the fight. J fished Sue's pyjamas out of the crack between the sofa and the bed, and Sue shared out the bedclothes in a friendly, sisterly way. J put out the light.

'Good night, sleep tight, mind the bugs don't bite,' said Sue.

'Shouldn't think I'll be able to sleep for laughing,' muttered J.

10

Sue did not sleep tight. She had a nightmare. Aunt Alice walked through the nightmare, shouting proverbs in her ear. Grandmother was behind her, with a butterfly net, trying to catch her. Mr Meier set his dog on her, and Sue was scared of Mr Joseph, because suddenly he was not a fat old dachshund any more, but a savage, gigantic hound. Then the manageress of the Chamois came and explained why Mother had to eat carrots and rusks because Grandmother had indigestion. The whole thing took place in a snow-covered meadow, and in the middle of the meadow stood a door saying PRIVATE. Sue wanted to reach the door because Benny was the other side, and he would save her from the huge dog and the butterfly net. But before she could get there the dog attacked her, and then Grandmother flung the butterfly net over both Sue and the dog.

Sue woke up. J was snorting like a horse, making a horrible noise. Sue reached across and grabbed the corner of J's pillow. She tugged it, and J stopped snorting and snuffling. Sue let go of the pillow.

She lay still. She could hear someone whistling out in the road. They were whistling *Colonel Bogey*. That must be Benny. She put one leg out of bed, felt around on the floor with her foot, and met something soft and woolly. She dug her toes into the soft, woolly thing and fished it up on the bed. Good, it was her sweater! Fishing about with her toes again, Sue retrieved her socks, blouse and ski pants and put them on underneath the bedclothes. Then she got out of bed and crawled around the floor looking for her boots. There was one. And there was the other. Unfortunately they turned out to be J's boots. 'Bother!' muttered Sue. She didn't want to put the light on and wake J; J wouldn't understand her wanting to go for a walk at night. Finally Sue found her own boots. Now for a cap, any cap. She found one in the crack between the sofa and the bed. With J's check cap on her uncombed hair, Sue tiptoed out of the room.

The corridor and the pine staircase were both lit up. Sue crept downstairs and over to the front door of the Green Chamois. The door was locked. Sue was puzzled. Benny had been whistling out in the street—it *had* been Benny, surely? Sue went into the dining room, which was dark, though a faint beam of light from the hall fell into it. The tables with their white cloths looked like fat ghosts. Sue made her way past the fat ghosts to one of the windows, and pulled back the check curtains. She cleared an asparagus fern, two cacti and a small rubber plant off the sill, only to find the catch of the window was jammed and nothing she could do would shift it. Sue went to the next window, took two pots of geraniums and a flowering thorn off the sill and tried that one. This time the catch was not jammed. Sue opened it. She estimated that the distance between the sill and the road was about one metre seventy. I can jump that, thought Sue. She jumped, landing safely enough, though not on her feet. The road outside the Green Chamois was covered with ice and smooth as glass. She sat on the icy road, wondering how many bruises she'd have to show for it next day. And where was Benny? The road was empty. Sue stood up, buttoned her jacket and pulled the check cap down over her ears. She was scared. Maybe that had not been Benny whistling *Colonel Bogey* after all. Other people could

know the same tune. She did not know how late it was,
but she did know it was easy enough to jump one metre
seventy down, not so easy to jump back up again. Of
course, she could ring the Green Chamois's front door
bell, but she didn't want to do that except as a last resort.
Sue decided to wait. Leaning against the wall, she made
up poetry to pass the time. She muttered:

'The white mist swirls round my head,
the Sergeant-Major is in my bed.
Come on, Benny, do!
Come on, this isn't very nice.
I don't want to spend all night on the ice!
Come on, Benny, do!
My nose is freezing and so are my ears,
They'll soon freeze off if nobody hears.
Come on, Benny, do!
I'm out here all on my own.
I'm too young to be out alone.
Come on, Benny, do!'

Sue's muttered invocation obviously worked, because
someone emerged from the mist, whistling. It was Benny.
'Hi, Sue,' said Benny. 'What are you doing here?'
'I thought you whistled for me.'
Benny, it turned out, had been whistling not for Sue but
for Mr Joseph. 'I've been running round after him for the
last hour,' said Benny. 'His inside's all upset. He ate far
too much yesterday, greedy old dog.'
Sue realized that she herself had eaten far too little
yesterday. 'I'm hungry,' she said.
Benny pointed into the mist, and said there was a coffee
bar open.
'Can we go to a coffee bar in the middle of the night?'
asked Sue.
'Why not?' said Benny. 'Anyway, it isn't the middle of

the night, it's five-thirty in the morning.'

'Have you got any money?'

Benny said he had plenty to get Sue something to eat.

It was lovely and warm in the coffee bar. There was no one there but the girl behind the counter, who was knitting the roll-neck on a gigantic pullover. She said it was a Christmas present for her fiancé.

'Your fiancé must be very big,' said Sue.

The girl behind the counter described her fiancé to Sue, in detail. Altogether he seemed to be a remarkable man. Sue was enthralled. She ate four sausages and drank three glasses of apple juice and listened to the girl behind the counter. Then a man came into the coffee bar. Benny knew him; he was the local butcher. The butcher said he just had time for a cup of coffee, because his wife's coffee was so horrible, and then he had to take half a pig to the inn in the next village. Benny asked the butcher if he and Sue and Mr Joseph could come too, and he said yes.

'Right, let's get moving,' he told them.

The next village was some way off. It was warm in the butcher's van, and the engine rumbled in a comforting way as the headlights tried to penetrate the mist. 'Real old pea-souper!' grumbled the butcher.

Suddenly a figure emerged from the fog, waving, and the butcher braked. 'Why, that's our teacher!' he said.

Sure enough, the village schoolteacher had driven her car into the ditch. Sue liked to see a teacher look silly; so did Benny. They clambered out of the van after the butcher. Mr Joseph took no interest, but rolled himself up into a ball on the seat of the van.

The poor teacher was frozen and frantic. Her car had been stuck in the ditch for an hour. With Benny's help, the butcher started a rescue operation. They fetched a rope from the van, the butcher tied it to the teacher's car and then to the back of his van. Meanwhile Sue was asking the teacher if she had a driving licence, and got a savage glare in return.

The butcher got back in his van and started up. 'Here goes!' he shouted.

The rope stretched taut. Benny shouted well-intentioned advice to the teacher through the window of her car. Sue stood and watched, enjoying herself. The teacher looked just like a schoolgirl doing a very difficult arithmetic test.

'Keep going, keep going!' shouted the butcher. The teacher's car gave two little jerks and then one violent jerk. Sue thought it was about to tip over.

It did not tip over; it was back on the road again. The butcher untied the rope, and the teacher thanked him. 'You're welcome, miss! Just give my little Hans an A for arithmetic some time!'

The teacher said she was sorry, she was afraid Hans had got a D for his last test again.

By the time the butcher got back in his van the sun was rising and the mist had cleared. 'Soon be there!' the butcher said.

The shops were open in the next village, and there were a good many people out in the street. The butcher stopped outside the inn and hooted. The landlord and his son came out and helped the butcher get their half pig into the house. 'You two wait here. Shan't be a minute,' the butcher told Benny and Sue.

He was several minutes. Sue and Benny waited. 'What's the time?' asked Sue.

'Past eight-thirty,' groaned Benny.

'Oh, lord!' muttered Sue. She realized Mother and Grandmother would have gone down to breakfast ages ago.

'Go and find the butcher!' Sue told Benny. Benny did not want to. 'Benny, they'll all be furious if we're late!' Sue said. 'And that won't do Operation Marriage much good.'

Benny said nothing for a moment. Then, reluctantly, he said, 'Look, Sue, you know I have a feeling Operation Marriage won't come off anyway. I didn't know my dad disliked your mother so much.'

'Doesn't he like her at all, then?'

'He was saying yesterday evening how the mere sight of her threatened to give him a peptic ulcer.'

Sue kept quiet. What was there to say?

'He doesn't like women at all,' said Benny. 'Not since my mother went off.'

'Where did she go?'

'France,' said Benny. 'I can remember her going away. I yelled for her to take me too.'

'And did she?'

Benny grinned. 'Don't be daft! Would I be here if she had?'

Sue nodded.

Benny said, 'Anyway, she and the man she went off with have got three babies now.'

'Then you've got brothers and sisters!' cried Sue.

'No, I haven't,' said Benny.

Sue would have liked to ask more about the three babies, but the butcher came back, and it was none of his business.

'Home we go,' said the butcher.

It was ten to ten when Sue and Benny got out of the butcher's van. Sue did not in the least want to go into the Chamois. Grandmother would kick up a fuss because Sue had not been there at breakfast. Mr Meier didn't like Mother. Aunt Alice might well be still quoting proverbs that had nothing to do with anything, and J would probably be cross too.

'Come on, don't be such a coward,' said Benny. Mr

121

Joseph barked encouragingly.

The manageress was standing in the hall of the Chamois. She, for one, was delighted. 'So here come our little runaways!' she said, and she made for the kitchen to get Sue and Benny some breakfast.

J came out of the dining room.

'Anything up?' asked Sue.

J groaned. 'Anything up? *Anything up*? I'll say there is!'

Sue, J and Benny went into the dining room, which was empty. Benny asked, 'Well, what is it?' He sat down at a table. 'They don't have to carry on, we're not tiny any more. We can go for a walk without asking permission first, can't we?'

'*That* wasn't it,' said J. 'They only got a little bit worked up about that, and then the really awful part happened.'

'*What* awful part?' asked Benny and Sue in chorus.

'Well, Mr Meier and our family got to the dining room door at the same time, and the manageress was standing there. She pointed to a big table, and she said she'd laid it for all of us, because of course people who were such good friends as us and the Meiers would prefer to sit together at breakfast. Your father looked horrified, and Grandmother was shaking with fury, and Mother's eyelids were twitching like mad. And Aunt Alice got all mixed up again and shouted something about every man sticking to his last. But the manageress didn't notice, she was still talking, apologizing for the poky bedroom again and saying it was a pity Mr Meier hadn't booked three rooms for us in the first place.'

'Oh, no!' said Benny.

Sue put her left forefinger in her mouth and bit the nail, hard.

J went on. 'And that really did it! Your father said he had never booked any rooms for us at all, he wasn't fool enough to dig his own grave! And the manageress said but of course he had, he booked by telephone and she had sent a note of confirmation. And indeed if dear Mr Meier had *not* asked for rooms for us she couldn't have let us have them, because she gave regular visitors priority at Christmas. Then Mother said she booked the rooms through Mr Pribil. And the manageress said she had never heard of any Mr Pribil. They were all talking at the tops of their voices, but Grandmother was talking loudest of all. She said they were all trying to pull the wool over her eyes, but they couldn't hoodwink her, and she said she despised Mr Meier and Mother, she felt nothing but contempt for them.'

'Why Mother?' asked Sue.

'She thinks Mother arranged to meet Mr Meier at Stoder,' J explained. 'She said she'd been nourishing a snake in her bosom. She meant Mother.'

'What did my dad do?' asked Benny, anxiously.

'First he swore a lot,' said J. 'Then he said he had a fair idea what had happened, and it seemed he'd been rearing a second Brutus.'

'A second what?' said Sue.

Benny was looking very unhappy. He said, 'That'll be me. Brutus was the bloke who stabbed his father, Caesar.'

'And Aunt Alice's nerves really cracked up then,' J went on, 'and she had an awful attack of proverbs. She walked up and down shouting, "Too many cooks spoil the broth." She went on and on, and no one could calm her down till Mother got her out of the room, and now Grandmother's making cold compresses for her.'

The manageress brought Benny and Sue some breakfast, and asked J how Aunt Alice was, and if the poor soul was feeling better. 'Not that I mind it today, when there aren't so many guests,' she added. 'But by tomorrow the place will be full, and if your poor auntie is still in such a state it will look rather funny. Bad for business,

123

that's what!'

Mr Meier appeared at the dining room door. He was not looking pleased. He told Benny to come up to their room, because he had a few words to say to him. Benny said what about his breakfast? Mr Meier said never mind his breakfast. Reluctantly, Benny got up. At this moment a large sky-blue object bowled into the dining room. Grandmother. Grandmother shouted that she would like Mr Meier to know he had no business talking to her granddaughters. First of all making overtures to her poor daughter, and now these poor innocent children! It was disgusting behaviour, and as for her poor sister Alice, he had driven her to a nervous breakdown!

While Grandmother shouted, she was glaring at Mr Meier and stamping her left foot furiously on the floor. Unfortunately, she brought it down on Mr Joseph's tail. Mr Joseph might be old and fat and asthmatic, but this was too much for him. He yelped, pulled his poor tail away, jumped up and bit Grandmother in the calf. Mr Joseph's teeth were not what they used to be, but all the same he drew blood.

'Oh dear, oh dear!' wailed the manageress of the Chamois. 'Such a good little dog in the usual way!'

Mr Joseph slunk under the table.

'It wasn't his fault,' said Benny. 'The old bag trod on him!'

Grandmother stared at her leg. Her sky-blue sock was getting redder every moment. Grandmother gasped, 'Mr Meier, we shall see each other in court!'

Then Grandmother limped out of the dining room.

Benny dragged Mr Joseph out from under the table and inspected his tail. It seemed to be all right.

'Benny,' said Mr Meier, 'you've been led astray, but I forgive you! Come on, we're leaving!'

'But Dad . . .' said Benny.

'Oh, Mr Meier, do be reasonable!' cried the manageress.

Mr Meier said he was being very reasonable: he did not want the murder of Grandmother on his conscience on Christmas Eve, he'd rather have some peace and quiet, and naturally he would pay for his room until January 3rd, because he knew it wasn't the manageress's fault.

Then he took his son's shoulder and steered him out of the dining room. The manageress followed them, making soothing remarks which did not soothe anyone.

J took over the remains of Benny's breakfast. Munching, she muttered:

'Eight little Indians thought Stoder would be
heaven,
Aunt Irma went to the Tirol, and then there were
seven.
Seven little Indians didn't really mix,
Mr Meier hates Grandmother, so then there were
six.
Six little Indians, that dachshund made a dive
At Granny; Benny had to go, and then there were
five.'

'How's it going on?' Sue asked. J shrugged her shoulders and made a face. 'We'll have to wait and see, Sue,' she said.

Sue and J did not feel like going to their room. Still less did they feel like going to Mother's or Grandmother's rooms. Nor did they want to go for a walk, in case they missed seeing what happened next. So they stayed in the dining room, and the manageress brought them apple juice and almond biscuits and a running commentary on the latest developments.

'Fancy that!' said the manageress. 'Those poor city folks, with their nerves in such a state. But a good little dog like Mr Meier's can't bite people very often. Dear me, I don't know why your granny had to make so much noise! And now I've had to phone the doctor to come and look at your granny's leg!'

'Fancy that!' said the manageress, later. 'Mr Meier is really going! He's paid his bill, and their cases are down in the hall. Poor Mr Meier, his nerves are in a bad way too! And that poor lad! Standing by their luggage looking quite glum!'

'Fancy that!' said the manageress. 'The doctor just came, and I took him up to your granny. Dear me, I do hope the doctor doesn't say that poor old dog might have rabies!'

'What would happen if he does think Mr Joseph might have rabies?' asked Sue.

The manageress was not sure, but she thought it would mean trouble for Mr Joseph as well as Grandmother.

'Fancy that!' said the manageress. 'The doctor's just gone, and he said to me, "Call that a dog-bite?" he said. "Why, it only grazed the lady's skin! Calling a doctor out just for that! As if I didn't have more urgent cases on my hands!" Yes, that's what the doctor said.'

The manageress poured out more apple juice and put another plate of almond biscuits on the table. She went on, 'But then there's the other lady, your poor dear great-auntie, now the doctor said she was really poorly, her nerves were in a shocking state, he said. A most remarkable case, that's what the doctor said, but being only a country GP, he said, he didn't think it was within his province. It needed a specialist, that's what he said.'

Then the manageress said, well, she must see about lunch now, she couldn't stand here chatting all day when there were the potatoes to peel and the carrots to scrape and the meat to cut up.

'Can we help peel potatoes?' asked Sue. 'You see, we don't have much else to do.'

The manageress said yes, of course she could do with a couple of willing helpers, but she pointed out that the sun was shining outside, and they could go walking up behind the hotel, and there was a pretty little Christmas crib outside the church.

Sue and J preferred to peel potatoes. They followed the manageress into the kitchen.

Sue and J peeled three kilos of potatoes and cleaned and scraped two kilos of carrots, and chopped half the carrots up. And they sliced eight celeriac roots into thin slices. The manageress told them how helpful they were, which was nice; it seemed to be some time since anyone had praised Sue and J. The manageress said she wished she had two good, handy daughters like them, and she told them all about her son, who was studying medicine in Innsbruck, but he was coming home this afternoon and staying till Twelfth Night. Then the hotel porter càme into the kitchen and said, 'Missus, you know the blue lady that got bitten by that dog? She's outside wanting her bill. She says she and the other lady need their own doctor at home to look after them.'

J dropped her vegetable knife. Sue jumped so violently that she cut her little finger. The manageress wiped her hands on a teacloth and said, 'Just you tell the ladies they shall have their bill directly.'

'Right,' said the porter, and he went out.

The manageress sat down at the kitchen table, got her glasses and a little pad out of the drawer, and put her glasses on.

'Well now,' she said. 'They didn't give us the pleasure of their company for long.' And she added, under her breath, 'And a good thing too. I can do without that sort of guest!'

'Can we have Grandmother's room back now?' asked Sue. The manageress nodded. Then she got up and went out of the kitchen with Grandmother's bill. Sue whispered, 'Hey, J, everything's going to be all right! We've got our room back, and we'll be here on our own with Mother!'

'I don't believe it,' J whispered back. 'Nothing turns out right for us! Something else is bound to go wrong!'

There was much clattering and banging of cases out in the hall, and they could hear Grandmother saying, 'Watch what you're doing, please! My Christmas tree is in that box! Handle it carefully!'

They also heard the porter, grumbling, 'Coming for one day with as much luggage as if they were staying three years!'

Sue and J crept to the kitchen door. It was open, just a crack, and Sue and J looked carefully through that crack. They did not want Grandmother to see them. But anyway, Grandmother had no time to spare looking for her granddaughters: she had to count all the cases and boxes and cartons, and tell the reluctant porter what to do with them. And from time to time she had to feel her heavily bandaged leg. Now Aunt Alice was coming down the pine staircase. In her pink outfit. Her grey eyes were glowing dreamily, and she was smiling. 'We're going home,' she said. 'Columbus's egg, that's what it is, Columbus's egg!' She went over to Grandmother, patted her shoulder and repeated, 'Columbus's egg, Henrietta! We're going home!'

Grandmother tore her eyes away from the luggage and looked at her sister. 'Behave yourself, Alice!' she said. 'Go and sit in the car!'

Aunt Alice obediently left the Green Chamois. Sue and J left their lookout post at the kitchen door and ran to the window. They could see out into the street. Grandmother was just getting into the car.

'They're going! They really are going!' cried J. 'I didn't believe it till now!' She hugged Sue. Grandmother's car started up. Sue laughed. Sue chanted:

'Five little Indians on the first floor,
A dachshund bit Grandmother and then there were
four!'

J sang:

'Four little Indians, happy as could be,
Aunt Alice found Columbus's egg and then there
were three!'

Then she hugged her sister, and they danced a restrained dance of joy all round the the hotel kitchen, slapping their thighs and chanting:

'Eight little Indians thought Stoder would be
heaven,
Aunt Irma went to the Tirol, and then there were
seven.
Seven little Indians didn't really mix,
Mr Meier hates Grandmother, so then there were
six.
Six little Indians, that dachshund made a dive
At Granny; Benny had to go, and then there were
five.
Five little Indians on the first floor,
A dachshund bit Grandmother and then there were
four.
Four little Indians, happy as could be,
Aunt Alice found Columbus's egg and then there
were three!'

11

Suddenly Sue stopped dancing. She looked quite alarmed.

'What about Mother? Where's Mother? Why doesn't Mother come down?'

J looked alarmed too. 'Let's go and look in her room,' she said.

Sue followed J out of the kitchen. As they climbed the pine staircase J was muttering, 'I *knew* everything couldn't be all right. Nothing ever goes right. Not in our family. Mother must be furious with us, or she'd have come down by now.'

Sue said, 'Well, she can't be furious with you. You didn't do anything.'

'Try telling that to Mother!' muttered J.

J knocked at the door of Number 12. No answer. J asked, 'Mother! Mother? Are you in there?'

Still no answer. J turned the door handle and opened the door. Mother was lying on the bed. Lying on her back, staring at the ceiling. She was crying. It looked as if she'd cried a lot already; the hair round her ears was wet, and so was her pillow. Her nose was all red and swollen.

Sue went over to the bed and touched Mother's arm. 'What's the matter?' she asked.

Then Mother began trembling. Trembling all over. It was a dreadful sight, and her tears flowed even faster. Sue and J exchanged helpless glances. Sue felt confused. She had expected Mother to be cross, maybe even shout at them, but why was she crying like this? It was really too much to bear! Sue couldn't help it, she suddenly remembered how Mr Meier had described Mother—'fat and tearful and full of grievances'.

J was touching Mother's arm now. 'Stop it, Mother!' she begged. 'Do stop it!'

Mother did not stop it. She trembled harder than ever. Her lips quivered and the tears kept flowing.

Sue remembered J crying like that once, when the cat they had before Philip died. What had Mother done for J on that occasion? She'd undressed J and put her to bed, and given her a hanky to blow her nose and put a wet flannel on her forehead. And Mother had stroked J's hair and whispered, 'Don't worry, darling, it will all be all right.'

Could she do the same for Mother? She could try the flannel, anyway.

Sue went to the wash basin, turned on the tap and put Mother's big green face flannel under the cold water. She slapped the dripping flannel down on Mother's face. Thank goodness, it seemed to work! Mother trembled a little more and then lay still. Then she started to sob again, wailing in a hoarse and tearful voice that nobody liked her, nobody loved her, everybody hated her and no wonder, when she wasn't any good to anybody. She was ugly, and fat, and stupid! And cowardly. And she just brought bad luck to everyone, even her children, though she loved them so much. J tried to interrupt Mother. 'That's not true, Mother!' she cried. 'You're just telling yourself so, it isn't true!'

Mother went on sobbing. No, she said, it *was* true. It was her fault Aunt Alice had a nervous breakdown. And Grandmother didn't want anything more to do with her, and her sister would soon be getting married. Her own children despised her. The man she loved had left her.

Even her next door neighbour wouldn't eat in the same room as her.

Sue took the flannel off Mother's face. It felt lukewarm by now. Sue put it under the cold tap again and slapped it back on Mother's face. This time Mother kept quiet and lay perfectly still. She had stopped crying.

Sue took Mother's shoes off. She and J pulled the bedspread out from under Mother and covered her up. Sue pulled the check curtains across the window to darken the room, and she and J stood at the end of the bed and waited. After a minute or so they felt sure Mother had gone to sleep. They tiptoed out of the room and sat down on the top step of the pine staircase. Sue sighed. J sighed. 'Now what?' asked Sue.

J had closed her eyes and was biting her nails. She often closed her eyes when she was thinking; she said she thought better that way. And she always bit her nails when she was worked up. 'Why are you worked up?' Sue asked. 'What are you thinking?'

'Ssh,' said J. 'Keep quiet.'

Sue kept quiet, watching her sister think. J thought for a long time. Finally she took her fingers out of her mouth and opened her eyes. 'Come downstairs,' she said. 'I've got to make a phone call.'

'For the doctor?' asked Sue.

J shook her head.

'Who are you going to ring, then?'

J did not answer. She went down to the kitchen, where the phone was. The manageress was not there.

'Do you know the Vienna dialling code?' asked J. Sue did not, but there was a piece of paper pinned to the wall over the phone, with the telephone numbers of the butcher, the doctor, and the police station, and the Vienna dialling code was there too.

'Now, you just pray he's at home!' said J, dialling

a number.

'Who?' asked Sue.

'Father, of course,' said J.

It seemed about a hundred years before J finished dialling the eleven figures. 'It's ringing,' she whispered.

Sue did not pray. She thought: if Father is lying on the sofa with Philip on top of him, then now he'll be lifting Philip off and standing up. Now he'll be looking for his left slipper. And now he'll have found it. And now he'll be starting towards the phone.

Father moved faster than Sue expected. J was already saying, 'Hullo, Father. It's me, J.' Then she said, 'Yes, Sue's here too, beside me.'

Sue went as close as she could to J, but she couldn't make out what Father said. J was saying, 'Yes, we're here in Stoder. No, only Mother and Sue and me. Aunt Alice went very peculiar, and the Meiers' dog bit Grandmother.'

'No, not in Vienna, the Meiers' dog was here because Sue wanted Mr Meier and Mother to get married, but when he realized that—no, of course I don't mean the dog, I mean Mr Meier—well, then he went away. And Grandmother went away too because the dog bit her and she doesn't want anything to do with Mother any more. And Mother's in bed, and she's crying and trembling all over because she says nobody loves her. At least, she isn't crying at the moment, she's gone to sleep.'

J stopped talking, and listened, and nodded. Then she said, 'Oh yes, *yes*!' and hung up. She looked at Sue, smiling.

'He said he'd drive like the wind,' she told Sue.

'Drive where like the wind?' asked Sue.

'Here, idiot!' J laughed.

'But what will he do when he gets here?' asked Sue.

'Put things right, that's what he said,' J told her.

How long would it take to drive from Vienna to Stoder? Sue and J sat in the dining room trying to work it out. It wasn't easy. Would there be a lot of cars on the motorway, or almost none? Would Father stop for coffee? Would the waiter be quick bringing the coffee? Would Father take the Renault, or would he borrow Uncle Jonny's Alfa Romeo? Would he have to search the whole apartment for a tie before he started?

Well: suppose the motorway was crowded, and there was a minor accident holding up the traffic near Weiler, and Father stopped for coffee, and the waiter was a long time bringing it, and Father was driving the Renault, which could only do 140 k.p.h and even then only on the motorway, and the motorway only went as far as Salzburg, and if Father had to find his red tie, then it would take him about six hours, and he would reach Stoder about five in the afternoon.

But if Father didn't stop to look for his tie, and didn't stop for coffee, and borrowed the Alfa Romeo, and there wasn't much traffic, it might only take him three hours. So then he could be at the Green Chamois about two o'clock.

The manageress brought Sue and J their lunch herself, and asked how Mother was, and would she be coming down for lunch? J said Mother had gone to sleep because she was so tired.

'I'm not surprised,' said the manageress. 'All that carry-on with the old ladies!'

The manageress was in a bit of state herself, because she was expecting her son to arrive soon, and he drove so fast that she was a little worried about him. After lunch the manageress showed Sue and J her son's Christmas presents. Sue thought he was getting a lot of presents. They were all in the manageress's own room; he was going to get a stereo system, a fur coat, a wallet with several large notes in it, and a pile of records and pullovers and shirts and books, a fur cap with a fox's brush on it, a camera and a mini-refrigerator for chilling a bottle of whisky. The manageress was very proud of this pile of presents, though she had not chosen them herself. A friend of her son's had chosen them for her because, said the manageress, she didn't know what the fashion was these days.

She had a Christmas tree in her room too: a wonderful big Christmas tree, hung with gingerbread cookies and stars made of woven straw, and gilded nuts and red apples. 'Oh, we always have a tree,' she said. 'However old my lad gets, he has to have a tree, or he says he wouldn't come home!'

Sue envied the manageress's son slightly. Not because of the pile of presents: because of the Christmas tree, and the manageress herself.

'Don't stare!' whispered J. 'Let's go and wake Mother up. It's past one o'clock.'

'Oughtn't we to let her sleep?' said Sue. 'We can wake her up when Father gets here.'

'No, she'll want to tidy herself up so she looks right,' J explained.

'How will she want to look?'

'Pretty, of course, so Father will like her!'

At last Sue grasped just what J was planning, and how she thought Father would put everything right. Sue shook her head.

'But Mother doesn't want Father any more,' she pointed out.

'Well, if that's what you think, you're off your head!' said J.

'But she said so!'

'Well? People say lots of things they don't mean.'

Sue shook her head again. She said, 'And Father doesn't want Mother any more.'

'Did he say so?' asked J.

'No,' said Sue, 'but people sometimes think things they don't say.'

'Well, *I* think,' said J, raising the first two fingers of her right hand as if she were about to take an oath, '*I* think Mother still loves Father, and Father still loves Mother. And anyway people can live happily together upon a basis of mutual respect even in the absence of passionate desire.'

'What?' said Sue.

'I read that in the agony column of the paper,' said J.

'Oh,' said Sue.

Sue and J went into Mother's room without knocking; it was high time to break with the habits of the Buchinger household. Mother was not asleep any more, but she was still in bed. Her eyelids were swollen, and lay over her reddened eyes like two fat caterpillars. Her nose was red and swollen too. Father won't think much of her looking like that, thought Sue.

'What is it?' asked Mother, in a faint, weary voice. Her arms were hanging limply by her sides. I really don't want to be unfair, thought Sue, but she's sounding like someone in a film again.

'Father will be here soon,' said J. 'He's on his way. Driving like the wind, he said.'

Mother sat up. Her voice was not faint or weary any more, and she certainly didn't sound like someone in a film. 'Who?' she said. 'Father? Coming here? How? When? Why?'

J said, 'He's coming because I rang him up, and we can't go on like this, and it isn't true that nobody loves you!'

Mother leaped out of bed and ran to the mirror. 'Oh, my goodness, whatever do I look like!' she cried.

She turned the taps on, put both hands under the stream of water and started splashing it into her poor

136

swollen face. She wailed into the water, 'Oh, good heavens, my hair! What a mess! Get my black trousers out of my case!' she called to J. 'And my sweater, the one with the spots on!'

J got Mother's black trousers and green sweater out of the case. 'Father doesn't like the spotted sweater,' she said.

Sue sat on the bed. 'Well, honestly!' she muttered to herself, viewing the scene in amazement. Mother had stopped splashing her face with water and was chasing about the room. She grabbed another sweater from her case, cried, 'Oh, it doesn't fit!' threw it on the bed, tried the next one, discarded that too. In between she was looking for a clean pair of tights and tearing off the clothes she was already wearing.

J was dashing up and down too, sounding like a cackling hen. 'Put your mauve eyeshadow on!' she cackled. 'Did you bring your ruby brooch? What about your striped hostess skirt?'

Sue was amazed. Fancy Mother having a striped hostess skirt and a ruby brooch and mauve eyeshadow here!

J was crawling under the bed to see if she could find Mother's other green shoe. Mother was standing in the middle of the room, her right foot in its partner, which was very high-heeled. She looked lop-sided. Her black, blue and green striped hostess skirt hung from her lopsided hips. It hung limply because part of her slip had got stuck in the zip, and now the zip would neither open nor close. 'It's stuck!' Mother was crying frantically. 'It's stuck!'

Mother had nothing at all on her top half, since she hadn't decided on a sweater yet. She had a roller with hair wound round it dangling in front of each ear, to help her tears dry out properly. Oddest of all were Mother's eyes.

137

One looked the same as usual, only rather swollen; the other had a heavy blue streak of eyeliner and lots of mauve eyeshadow on the lid.

Before Mother could make up the other eyelid, or J could find the other green shoe, the bedroom door opened. There was Father, standing in the doorway, staring at Mother. J sighed, 'He drove *faster* than the wind!'

Father was still staring at Mother. He took a step into the room, closed the door behind him, and went on staring. Then he started to laugh. A loud, ringing laugh. He couldn't stop. Tears of laughter filled his eyes and ran down his cheeks.

'Don't you dare laugh!' snapped Mother.

'I'm not laughing,' groaned Father, 'ho, ho, I'm not laughing, really, ha, ha, I *won't* laugh, ho, ho!' Father wiped the tears of laughter from his eyes with the back of his hand, still chuckling.

'If you go on laughing I shall *hit* you!' said Mother. But she did not sound as if she meant it.

Father went towards Mother. You could see he was trying to keep back a fresh burst of laughter. Father took hold of both rollers and pulled them out of Mother's hair. Then he bent down and took the one high-heeled shoe off her foot.

'That's better!' he chuckled. 'Only you'll catch cold!'

Mother let out a little scream, and tried to cover her bare top half with her hands.

'You're mean!' she whispered, collapsing on Father's chest. Father patted her bare back gently and murmured, 'Yes, I know, I'm mean, I really am.'

'Come on!' J whispered to Sue.

Sue whispered back, 'No fear! This is just getting interesting. I'm staying.'

J took no notice of Sue; she tried to pull her out of the

room. 'Look, we've got to stay,' Sue whispered. 'Otherwise they'll do something silly again and everything will go wrong!'

'They will *not* do anything silly, and nothing will go wrong,' J assured Sue, tugging her sleeve. Reluctantly, Sue followed J out of the room.

Sue and J had been sitting outside the door of Number 12 for an hour. Sitting peacefully side by side. Now and then J nudged Sue in the ribs and said proudly, 'I did it!'

And Sue answered, without a trace of envy, 'Yes, you did it!'

After another half an hour, they both decided that the reconciliation had gone on long enough. Sue knocked gently at the door, and Mother came out. She had done her hair, and there was mauve eyeshadow on both eyelids. And her zip was done up properly, and of course she had a sweater on.

Mother said Father was having a little sleep, because he was tired after the journey. She sat down on the floor beside Sue and J, and said she had a problem.

'What, already?' cried J, horrified.

'No, not that sort!' said Mother. The problem was, Father had left in such a hurry he didn't have pyjamas or a toothbrush or a clean shirt with him. He was also wearing one blue sock and one red sock. And he was not quite sure if he'd locked the apartment door behind him. But the main thing was, he had been in such a hurry to leave that he had forgotten to take Philip the cat down to the caretaker. So there was poor Philip, all alone at home, unable to get his own cat food out of the fridge.

'And so we'll all have to go straight home,' said Mother.

Sue nodded. She repeated, 'So we'll all have to go straight home.' The word 'home' was sweet as raspberry ice melting in her mouth.

'Then what's the problem?' asked Sue.

'Well, we shan't get home till evening,' said Mother, 'so we won't be able to open our presents and have our Christmas Eve celebrations the same as usual.'

Sue and J began to laugh. They laughed so loud they woke Father, who came out of the bedroom in his one red sock and one blue sock.

'Did we wake you up?' asked Mother, full of concern.

'I feel wonderfully rested!' said Father. 'Well, how about starting for home?'

'You'll have to pay the bill first, Fred,' said Mother.

More Beaver Books

On the following pages you will find some other exciting Beaver Books to look out for in your local bookshop

BUT JASPER CAME INSTEAD

Christine Nostlinger

It was Tom who was supposed to go and stay with the family in Vienna. But Jasper went instead. And, as thirteen-year-old Ewald and his sister Billie were soon to find out, Jasper was quite a handful. He didn't like washing, for a start. Or the food. And he certainly didn't want to go on outings.

How the family deal with disaster on disaster makes for a hilarious – and moving – story.

If you're an eager Beaver reader, perhaps you ought to try some more of our exciting titles. They are available in bookshops or they can be ordered directly from us. Just complete the form below and enclose the right amount of money and the books will be sent to you at home.

☐	THE SUMMER OF THE WAREHOUSE	Sally Bicknell	£1.25
☐	THE GOOSEBERRY	Joan Lingard	£1.25
☐	FOX CUB BOLD	Colin Dann	£1.50
☐	GHOSTLY AND GHASTLY	Barbara Ireson Ed.	£1.50
☐	WHITE FANG	Jack London	£1.25
☐	JESS AND THE RIVER KIDS	Judith O'Neill	£1.50
☐	A PATTERN OF ROSES	K. M. Peyton	£1.25
☐	YOU TWO	Jean Ure	£1.50
☐	SNOWY RIVER BRUMBY	Elyne Mitchell	£1.25

If you would like to hear more about Beaver Books, and discover all the latest news, don't forget the BEAVER BULLETIN. If you just send a stamped self-addressed envelope to Beaver Books, Brookmount House, 62-65 Chandos Place, Covent Garden, London WC2N 4NW, we will send you the latest BULLETIN.

If you would like to order books, please send this form, and the money due to:

HAMLYN PAPERBACK CASH SALES, PO BOX 11, FALMOUTH, CORNWALL, TR10 9EN.

Send a cheque or postal order, and don't forget to include postage at the following rates: UK: 55p for first book, 22p for second, 14p thereafter; BFPO and Eire: 55p for first book, 22p for second, 14p per copy for next 7 books, 8p per book thereafter; Overseas: £1.00 for first book, 25p thereafter.

NAME ....

ADDRESS ....

....

Please print clearly